—— The Roman —

FROM OSTIA
TO ALEXANDRIA
WITH FLAVIA GEMINA

find out more about the Roman Mysteries,
visit www.romanmysteries.com

THE ROMAN MYSTERIES
by Caroline Lawrence

The Roman Mysteries

FROM OSTIA
TO ALEXANDRIA
WITH FLAVIA GEMINA

Caroline Lawrence

Orion
Children's Books

First published in Great Britain in 2008
by Orion Children's Books
a division of the Orion Publishing Group Ltd
Orion House
5 Upper St Martin's Lane
London WC2H 9EA
An Hachette Livre UK Company

1 3 5 7 9 10 8 6 4 2

A catalogue record for this book is
available from the British Library

Printed in Great Britain by Clays Ltd, St Ives plc

ISBN 978 1 84255 665 8

www.orionbooks.co.uk
www.romanmysteries.com

To my husband Richard
who hardly ever complains

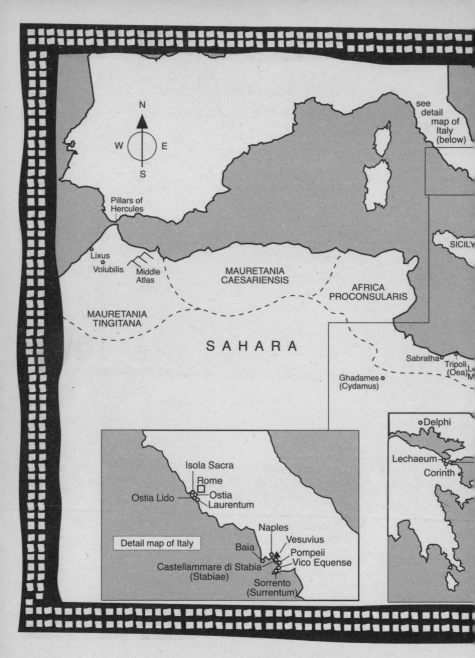

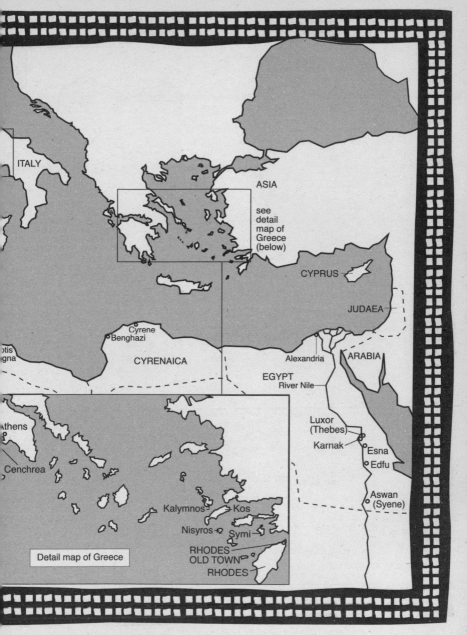

ITALY

ASIA

see
detail
map of
Greece
(below)

CYPRUS

JUDAEA

Cyrene
Benghazi

otis
gna

CYRENAICA

Alexandria

ARABIA

EGYPT
River Nile

Luxor
(Thebes)
Karnak

Esna

Edfu

Aswan
(Syene)

thens

Cenchrea

Kalymnos

Kos

Nisyros

Symi

Detail map of Greece

RHODES
OLD TOWN

RHODES

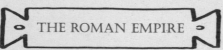

THE ROMAN EMPIRE

CONTENTS

INTRODUCTION

If you are between eight and fourteen years old, you might know that I write a detective series for children set in first century Rome. The series is called *The Roman Mysteries* and it features four children who become friends and have adventures during the reign of the Emperor Titus (AD 79-81). Flavia Gemina is a highborn Roman girl, Jonathan ben Mordecai is her Jewish neighbour, Nubia her beautiful slave-girl, and Lupus is a tongueless mute whom they first find living wild in the graveyard outside their home town of Ostia, the port of Rome. Together the four solve mysteries centred around real historical events and people.

Some people think that because I write detective stories I am clever and observant. The reality could not be further from the truth. Because I'm a daydreamer, I forget people's names, can't remember faces, and often fail to notice huge differences in some of my closest friends: things like different hair colour, new glasses and drastic weight loss.

I also have a total block about cars. Except for E-type Jaguars and SmartCars, they all look the same to me. If the police asked me for the description of a car that caused an accident, I would probably say, 'Um . . . it was silver?'

That's why I admire fictional detectives like Sherlock Holmes, Nancy Drew and Adrian Monk so much. They really see and remember the details. And that's why I created my own fictional detectives: to be clever.

Flavia Gemina is the sort of person I would like to be. Clever, observant and with a good eye for detail. Her friend Jonathan is literate in the most practical sense: he speaks several languages and knows at least three alphabets. Nubia is intuitive. She senses if something's wrong, even if she can't put her finger on exactly why. And Lupus is good at sneaking, spying, eavesdropping and generally making himself invisible. A good detective needs all these qualities. He or she needs to be observant, literate, intuitive and good at following people around.

Writers of historical fiction are like detectives. We have to recreate the scene of the crime, i.e. the past. Our clues are the ancient artefacts they used. Our witnesses are the writings of people who lived long ago, in my case: two thousand years. Over time, I've discovered a third way of reconstructing the past. By looking for it in different countries.

A famous first line from a book reads: 'The past is a foreign country . . .' I like to switch it around: 'A foreign country is the past . . .' Or it can be, if you know how to look.

In the countries that used to be part of the Roman Empire, some things haven't changed in two thousand years. Wild boar is still on the menu in Rome every year in February; starlings wheel at dusk in October; swifts return in May and umbrella pines release clouds of yellow pollen in that same month, dusting the SmartCars on the Via Veneto. In the hot summer months, you can sit at a table in the cool shade of an ancient plane tree and eat olives, a taste as old as cold water.

Today's Pompeian farmer digs with the same hoe as his first century ancestor. And his wife uses the same medicinal herbs that Pliny the Elder recommended in his *Natural History*. Inhabitants of the Greek island of Kalymnos bring votive plaques showing the parts of the body they want healed to the sacred grotto of a saint, just as their ancestors once brought clay models of body parts to the healer-god Asklepios. And an afternoon in a Moroccan hammam is probably very similar to a few hours spent in the Baths of Titus two thousand years ago. If you know where to look – if you know *how* to look – the past is visible everywhere.

This is not like any other travel book you will ever find. It will not tell you about exchange rates or which airlines travel to the places mentioned. But it will tell you how to find traces of the past in the places my books are set: Italy, Greece and North Africa. Together we are going to be detectives – like Flavia, Jonathan, Nubia and Lupus – and we will try to solve the question of what it would really have been like to live in the Roman Empire in the first century AD. To do this we are going to have to be observant, literate, intuitive and good at eavesdropping.

I am going to give you assignments and tasks. You might have to try a new type of food, learn a new alphabet and carefully observe the people around you. Most of all, you will have to use your imagination. That's something I am good at. And I'll bet you are, too.

FLAVIA'S TEN TIPS FOR STAYING SAFE WHEN YOU TRAVEL

1. Memorise the name of the hospitium (hotel) where you are staying.

2. Carry a piece of papyrus (paper) with your name and the address of where you are staying.

3. Take a carrier pigeon (mobile phone) to keep in touch with your parents if you are separated.

4. Try out your carrier pigeon (mobile phone) when you first arrive in the new country.

5. Most guidebooks have a few pages about the customs of different countries. (e.g. the thumbs-up sign means 'great' in many countries but in other countries it is rude!) Study these before you go.

6. Be polite, but don't trust anyone you don't know, especially people who invite you to go with them on your own.

7. Be alert! Watch out for suspicious behaviour, especially people following you.

8. If beggars or stallholders pester you, just smile politely and say 'no thank you'.

9. Do not go out without telling your parent or tutor and make sure you get their permission.

10. If you go out on your own, take a bodyguard or dog. (Or a parent or guardian.)

ITALY

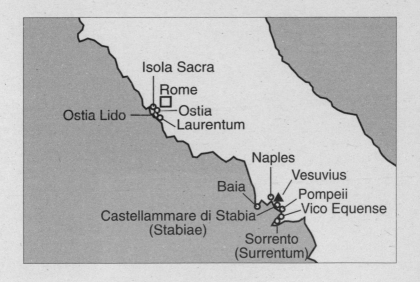

Isola Sacra
Rome
Ostia
Ostia Lido —
Laurentum

Naples
Vesuvius
Baia
Pompeii
Vico Equense
Castellammare di Stabia
(Stabiae)
Sorrento
(Surrentum)

ITALY

Most of the Roman Mysteries take place in Italy: Ostia, Rome and the Bay of Naples to be precise. I try to visit Italy at the time of year when each of my books is set, to get the feel of the place at different seasons. Sometimes I travel with my husband Richard, who does the maps in the books. Some times I travel on my own. The Roman Mysteries set in Italy are *The Thieves of Ostia (RM I)*, *The Secrets of Vesuvius (RM II)*, *The Pirates of Pompeii (RM III)*, *The Assassins of Rome (RM IV)*, *The Dolphins of Laurentum (RM V)*, *The Twelve Tasks of Flavia Gemina (RM VI)*, *The Enemies of Jupiter (RM VII)*, *The Gladiators from Capua (RM VIII)*, *The Sirens of Surrentum (XI)*, *The Charioteer of Delphi (RM XII)* and *The Slave-girl from Jerusalem (RM XIII)*.

MY FIRST RESEARCH TRIP TO OSTIA

THURSDAY 18 MAY 2000 – *London, England*
I am sitting in an Italian restaurant having my first lunch with my editor, Judith. One of my dreams has come true. She has agreed to publish six books in a series called the Roman Mysteries, all because of one manuscript: THE THIEVES OF OSTIA. *In fact, I am flying to Ostia that very evening for a one-day city break to Rome. Except I won't be going into Rome, I'll be staying near Rome's airport in order to visit Rome's ancient seaport. It will be my first visit to Ostia in over thirty years.*

I am a little dizzy from excitement (and from a glass of champagne) but a bitter espresso clears my head. I replace the tiny cup on the saucer, thank my new editor for a delicious lunch and tell her I must catch my flight. 'I hope you meet Flavia,' says Judith, as I turn to wave goodbye. 'What a strange thing to say,' I muse, walking out of the restaurant towards the underground.

FRIDAY 19 MAY 2000 – *Ostia Antica, Italy*
I am enjoying a very different lunch from yesterday's. I'm sitting in the ancient theatre of Ostia on a glorious spring day, sipping water and eating pistachio nuts. I've spent the morning wandering around the

site, soaking up the atmosphere while taking photos and making notes in a notebook. (Ever since I decided to become a writer I have been buying pocket-sized notebooks in different colours. This one just happens to be grape-coloured.)

Suddenly, I spy a group of Italian schoolgirls skipping rope on the stage. My eye is drawn to one of the girls: slightly fairer than the others and a bit of a tomboy. My editor's words come back to me: 'I hope you meet Flavia.' I put down my pistachio nuts and sit up straight. It's her. It's Flavia!

Dare I take a photo?

'Carpe diem,' I say to myself. 'Seize the day'. I take a deep breath and approach the girls, whose teachers are safely nearby. In very rudimentary Italian, I try to explain that I am writing a book about a Roman girl who lives here in Ostia. The girls swarm around me, chattering happily. Then I ask if I can take a photo. I get some group shots and one girl snaps me with the others. I also take a picture of 'Flavia' on her own. Her name is Francesca and she gives me a wonderful smile.

When I got back to London, I used the photo of Francesca as a model for a drawing of Flavia, and it became her mosaic portrait on the front cover of the books.

FLAVIA

Ever since then I have tried to travel to the places I write about, in order to get the feel of the place and be inspired. In this book I am going to share excerpts from my notebooks. If you have read my books, you will immediately see when and where and how I get lots of my ideas.

TWELVE TASKS TO DO
IN AND AROUND OSTIA
(FROM EASY TO CHALLENGING):

1. Hug an umbrella pine.

2. Find the mosaic of four mules Pudes, Podagrosus, Potiscus and Barosus.

3. Find the elaborately curled wig of marble – made to fit on the bust of a Flavian lady – in the Ostia Museum.

4. Buy a black and white mosaic kit from the bookshop.

5. Have a photo of yourself taken in front of the ancient latrines.

6. Pretend you are a blindfolded donkey, and walk round and round a millstone in one of the bakeries.

7. Sketch the mosaic of the elephant with the inscription STAT SABRATENSIVM above it.

8. Find the synagogue and imagine the shoreline being where the road is now.

9. Locate the approximate site of Flavia's house (still unexcavated) and read a favourite passage of the Roman Mysteries.

10. Have Sunday lunch at *Allo Sbarco di Enea* – the cheesy but fun restaurant just outside the site – and have a photo of yourself taken with a waiter in a short tunic.

11. Find a mosaic of Ostia's lighthouse among the tombs of the Isola Sacra.

12. Find the crayfish mosaic in the so-called Villa of Pliny in Laurentum.

OSTIA LIDO

EXCERPTS FROM THE
GRAPE-COLOURED NOTEBOOK:

FRIDAY 19 MAY 2000 – *Ostia Lido*
6.00am – *five stray cats: two black three tortoiseshell by a kiosk … Full moon palest apricot – three fingers above the milky sea … Seagulls at one level, swifts at a higher … Little brown sparrow? White collar, dark head pecking in the soft sand … Offshore breeze doesn't smell salty*
7.15am – *set breakfast at the Hotel Ping Pong. Espresso, croissant, juice – a Beatles' song on the sound system …*
9.00am – *off to catch the bus to Ostia Antica …*
6.00pm – *(back at Ostia Lido) Incredibly stiff offshore breeze coming from the west. The breakers aren't very tall but they're very foamy and frothy. The water has so much sand in it that it looks brown … I can hear canvas flapping madly: awnings and umbrellas. Flags are cracking in the wind. How did ancient sailors manage? …*

SATURDAY 20 MAY 2000 – *Ostia Lido*
7.00am – *it's funny how on my second day here, everything is already familiar: the seafront, the feral cats by the kiosk, the buildings, the tiny espresso … even the same Beatles' song at breakfast …*

· QUESTION ·
WHICH ROMAN MYSTERY BEGINS WITH
THE FOUR FRIENDS ON THE
BEACH OF OSTIA?
ANSWER: THE SECRETS OF VESUVIUS

A WALKING TOUR OF OSTIA, THE ANCIENT PORT OF ROME

In the first century AD, Ostia was a bustling harbour town, with people from all over the Roman Empire: Greeks, Egyptians, Nubians, Syrians and Gauls. There would have been sailors, customs officers, garrisons of soldiers, merchants selling their wares, criminals on the run, and of course the storehouse owners and bakers to manage the grain. Ostia was the breadbasket of Rome. The harbour of Portus, a few miles north, is where the big grain ships from Egypt docked. Grain was stored in Ostia's many warehouses and then transported up to Rome by road or barge along the winding Tiber.

Today, Ostia is not as well preserved as Pompeii, but in its own way it's just as impressive. You can see traces of frescoes on the walls, half standing columns, marble thresholds, millstones from bakeries, and Ostia's distinctive black and white mosaics. Because Ostia is off the tourist track it can be extraordinarily peaceful. Get there early, or linger in the evening. Go in the spring or autumn and you can wander undisturbed around the remains of baths, temples, houses, shops, taverns, latrines and even the theatre without seeing more than a party of Italian schoolchildren in the distance.

The gates open at 9.30am and you should allow an hour to get there, if you are coming from Rome. Wear a sunhat and trainers, and dress in layers; the weather on the coast is changeable. Take the metro's Linea A to the stop called *Piramide*, then take the train destination *Laurentina*

10

the rest of the way. Make sure you get off at Ostia Antica (Ancient Ostia), the stop before Ostia Lido (Ostia Beach).

N.B. Just remember: don't come on Mondays. That's the one day of the week it's closed.

The first thing you notice about Ostia even before you buy your ticket at the kiosk and enter the site are the umbrella pines. Today, there are thousands of these beautiful trees in and around Ostia, making it one of the greenest suburbs of Rome. The umbrella pine – *pinus maritimus* – was a striking feature of the Italian coast even in Roman times. In a famous letter, Pliny the younger described the cloud of ash that emerged from Vesuvius as looking like an umbrella pine: a trunk-like column of smoke rising up and then flattening out at the top. Flavia, Jonathan and Nubia catch their first glimpse of Lupus when he is trapped up one of these Ostian pines by some wild dogs.

Romans were not allowed to bury their dead within the city so they placed graves along main roads right up to the town walls. The tombs are the first thing you'll

---

It was not a proper tomb because there was no body. Jonathan had died in the terrible fire in Rome a month before and his body was buried in a mass grave with hundreds of others.

Back home in Ostia, the port of Rome, Jonathan's father had paid a stonemason to inscribe Jonathan's name on the family tomb. But it was with other Jewish tombs on the Isola Sacra, almost three miles away.

Nubia and her friends wanted Jonathan's memorial to be closer.

That was why they had crept out one moonlit night take a disused marble block from beside Ostia's synagogue. The sun was rising by the time they eased the heavy stone off the borrowed handcart. (RM VIII, p 3)

see when you enter the site of Ostia. It is among the tombs that Flavia and her friends spy a suspected dog-killer. And it is here that they hold a memorial service for Jonathan, thinking he is dead.

In Flavia's time the Roman Gate would have been an impressive arch, faced with marble and flanked with statues of Victory and Minerva. Once you are 'inside' the town walls, you'll see a long stone water trough for the thirsty mules that pulled carts to and from Rome. Flavia once came here to hire a cart to Rome.

The Romans loved to spend an afternoon at the baths. There are at least a dozen different bath complexes in Ostia. The Cart Drivers' Baths are my favourite. This bath complex was exclusively for the muleteers who drove carts to and from Rome. Look for the delightful black-and-white mosaic of four mules with their names written beside them in Latin: Pudes (Modest), Podagrosus (Lame), Barosus (Dainty) and Potiscus (Tipsy).

> *The cart-drivers had their own tavern and stables just behind the trough, and their own baths complex across the road, but after they had bathed and filled their stomachs, this was where they waited for their next fare to Rome. (RM IV, p 45)*

In most Roman towns the main road was called the Decumanus Maximus. As at Pompeii, you can see the ruts made by a hundred thousand carts that carried grain and other goods to and from the port. Carry on up the Decumanus Maximus past the ancient shopping arcade towards the Baths of Neptune with their impressive mosaics of tritons and sea-nymphs. A

> *'Do you know what their names mean?' asked Flavia.*
> *'She does now,' said Feles with a grin, and leaned against*
> *the cart. 'Show us how Barosus walks.'*
> *Nubia handed Flavia the sun-hat and then minced along*
> *the road in dainty little steps. Flavia laughed.*
> *'And this is the Podagrosus,' said Nubia, coming back*
> *along the hot road with a heavy, exaggerated limp. 'And*
> *the Potiscus.' She staggered the last few steps as if she*
> *were tipsy. (RM IV, p 55)*

platform here gives a wonderful view of the whole site. Lupus runs down this road and almost knocks over a slave carrying a jar of urine to the fullers'.

Ostia's Theatre was one of the first buildings in Ostia to be excavated because its ruins were visible above ground. It would have seated two and a half thousand people in Flavia's day and has been heavily but accurately restored.

Located directly behind the theatre is The Forum of the Corporations. Built around a charming temple of Ceres, goddess of grain, this is where guilds or 'corporations' did business. Shaded by ancient umbrella pines, the delightful black-and-white mosaics illustrate the different offices. Ships and images of Ostia's famous lighthouse indicate ship owners or captains while baskets (modii) with their levelling rods are for grain-traders. My favourite mosaic is the elephant at the station of the beast importers from Sabratha. Flavia and her friends come here to interrogate a suspect.

> Around the grassy precinct of the temple was a
> three-storey colonnade which housed Ostia's various
> corporations. Flavia's father had once told Lupus that
> 'corporation' meant a group of people. There were the
> shipbuilders and owners; the tanners, rope-makers and
> sailors; the measurers and importers of grain; and the
> importers of other useful products: olive oil, wine,
> honey, marble and exotic beasts. (RM VI, p 60)

The main business centre of ancient Ostia was The Forum. Here the dominating landmark is a lofty brick building on a stepped platform. This is the Capitoleum, the temple to the Capitoline triad – Jupiter, Juno and Minerva. It would have been faced with marble to cover the brick. It is in the shadow of this temple that the evil Venalicius sells the beautiful Nubia.

The Basilica housed law-courts and magistrates' offices. Ostia's junior magistrate works here. Marcus Artorius Bato often helps the four with their

> Flavia had visited the offices on the first floor but she had
> never been on the vast ground floor of the basilica itself.
> Its lofty central nave was flanked by elegant columns of
> polished marble: pink veined with grey. The floor was
> made of highly polished marble, too: squares of inlaid
> apricot on creamy white. (RM XIII, p 116)

investigations. The basilica provides the location for an exciting courtroom scene in *RM XIII*, where the handsome young orator named Flaccus defends a mysterious and beautiful slave-girl who has been accused of triple homicide.

Opposite the Capitoleum are the remains of The Temple of Rome and Augustus. During the Saturnalia Flavia and Nubia find a clue in the face of the cult statue of Rome, personified as a beautiful Amazon.

> *In the Temple of Rome and Augustus, Rome was shown as a beautiful Amazon resting her foot on the world. (RM VI, p 137)*

While you're near the Forum, don't miss Ostia's most amusing landmark, the Roman toilets. Sitting right next to each other, with no dividing wall or doors, Romans would chat, gossip, extend and accept dinner invitations. The holes on top of the cool marble bench are for the obvious thing. The holes at the front are for the sponge-stick, ancient Roman toilet paper. Lupus has obviously never been here, or he'd know a sponge-stick is not for beating a drum.

Just past the Forum is a five-way crossroads. Crossroads were sacred places in Roman times and there was a temple where two lofty cypress trees stand today. Lupus makes some exciting discoveries here at the Shrine of the Crossroads one cold December dusk.

Near the museum (only open in the mornings) you can find a relatively well-preserved bakery. Grain was often converted to bread before it was transported, hence the many bakeries in Ostia. Notice the distinctive hourglass mills. These would have been operated by blindfolded donkeys. You can still see the circular trace of their hoof prints worn into the herringbone pattern of the brick floor.

> . . . a spacious room with two big millstones and one smaller one, all made of dark-grey stone. To Nubia the millstones looked like stout women with tightly belted waists. Around each one circled a blindfolded donkey.
> . . . 'The blindfold doesn't hurt,' said Porcius. 'It's to stop them getting dizzy. They go round and round all day. See how they're yoked to the beam?' He led Nubia to the smallest millstone. The others followed.
> (The Code of Romulus, p 12)

Built in the middle of the first century AD, Ostia's Synagogue is one of the oldest in the world. It's at the edge of the site, near the perimeter fence. The modern highway is exactly where the ancient shoreline would have been. All that's left of the synagogue today are a few pillars and blocks of marble. In the summer, swifts swoop in the warm air and you can see butterflies fluttering among the columns and minuscule red spider mites on the inscribed marble floor. Jonathan and his friends seek refuge in the synagogue when they are being chased by slave-dealers.

Make your way through the long grasses towards the Laurentum Gate. This would have been a quiet residential area of Ostia with houses dating from the time of Julius Caesar. You might find the Villa of Cartilia Poplicola, a young Roman widow who likes Flavia's father. Moving back towards the entrance of the site, parallel with the Decumanus Maximus, you'll find more storehouses, a fullers' (ancient laundry), and an underground Temple to Mithras.

What you won't find is Flavia's house. I made a conscious decision to have my characters live in an unexcavated part of the town. One day I hope they'll build a life-sized reconstruction, complete with Roman frescoes, fountains, mosaics, furniture and fittings. Until then, you can sit in the shade of an umbrella pine eating a snack and imagining that you are reclining in Flavia's triclinium.

If you haven't brought a snack, go to the modern cafeteria near the Museum. Here you can eat pasta or salad at a parasol-shaded table on a pleasant terrace only a stone's throw from the Tiber River. Nearby is the bookshop where you can buy guides to the ruins and souvenirs, such as a kit to make your own black-and-white mosaic of a dolphin.

Make sure you have a quick look in the Museum before it closes for the afternoon. There are a couple of fascinating portrait sculptures of boys and girls from Flavia's time.

After lunch, explore the site. Let your feet guide you. Lose yourself in Flavia's world. At the end of the day, investigate the medieval castle outside the ruins of Ostia, or take the train one stop to Ostia Lido and enjoy an ice cream at the beach.

OPTIONAL EXCURSIONS: LAURENTUM AND THE ISOLA SACRA

1. While you're in Ostia you might want to visit Pliny's villa at Laurentum (*RM II* and *RM V*). It's about four miles from the ruins of Ostia in the Castello Fusano nature reserve. The villa is marked by a modern brick arch. Look for black and white mosaics of sea-creatures. Even though this may not be Pliny's actual villa, a visit makes a pleasant day out. There are picnic benches, water fountains and lots of shady trees. There used to be an imperial elephant reserve here, and if you're lucky you might see a wild boar. Don't worry; they're very shy.

2. The Isola Sacra was one of Ostia's graveyards and has some of the best preserved Roman tombs in the world. There is a funeral here at the end of *RM XIII* and Jonathan comes here with Lupus at the beginning of *RM XIV.* Look out for the plaques in relief on some of the tombs: a midwife helping a woman give birth, a merchant ship, a donkey circling a millstone. The ancient site of Isola Sacra is a delightful place to wander and have a picnic, but check that it's open before you go.

DETECTIVE ASSIGNMENT I: FIRST IMPRESSIONS OF A NEW PLACE

What you will need: a pen or pencil and a pocket notebook. Every writer should carry a notebook for ideas, and every detective should carry a notebook for clues.

There is nothing like your first day in a new country. Everything is different. The smells, the sounds, the language, the air, the light, the birds, the animals, the cars, the street signs, the way the people dress and look, the whole flavour of the place.

For your first day, from the moment you get up, write down all that you observe. Write down what you have for breakfast. If you can, sit outside or by a window, and describe the people walking by: the people who live in this country. As you go through the day, write about the smells and sounds and tastes and all the things you see that strike you as funny or strange or different. Just for this first day, DO NOT TAKE PHOTOS. A camera makes you lazy. You point it at something interesting and think 'I can look at that more closely later when I get home.' But you never do. Later you can use a camera, but not this first day. (Unless you will not be coming back.)

You should write as much as you can on the first day because by the next day many things about this new place will *already seem familiar to you*.

ROME, THE ETERNAL CITY

Rome is an exciting but frustrating place. It is noisy, vibrant and crowded. But it is hard to see where the ancient Romans lived because Rome is still inhabited and people have built on top of the past. The famous Roman Forum is one of the most disappointing sites in the world. It is almost always crowded and in summer it's unbearably hot. At first glance it's just columns and rubble. Closer investigation doesn't make things much clearer. Several centuries of buildings piled on top of each other make it impossible to get a clear picture of what it would have been like. A few years ago I paid an expert guide to take me around and explain it. I still didn't understand it. Go there – so that you can say you have been – but there are better places in Rome to get a sense of what it was like two thousand years ago: the Colosseum, where there were beast-fights and gladiatorial combats; the Palatine Hill, where the Emperor lived; and the Tiber Island, which was a sanctuary devoted to the healing god Aesculapius.

A more unexpected place to find ancient Rome is the

medieval church of San Clemente, not far from the Colosseum. If you go inside, and follow the signs to the stairs leading down, you go back in time. You go down through the medieval period to the later Roman Empire. Finally you reach Nero's Rome. You can see how narrow some of the side streets were and you can even touch the brick walls.

TWELVE TASKS TO DO IN ROME (FROM EASY TO CHALLENGING):

1. Learn how to say 'hello', 'please', 'thank you' and 'toilets?' in Italian.

2. Find a first century Roman fountain, stop up the end with your thumb and see the jet of water arc out from the hole at the top! Drink some. It's safe!

3. Buy a replica Roman coin in the gift stall outside the Forum Romanum.

4. Find the round temple of Hercules in the Forum Boarium.

5. Have a therapeutic ice cream on the Tiber Island.

6. Go downstairs in the crypt of San
    Clemente and touch a wall from Nero's
    Rome.

7. Find the arch of Titus, built to commem-
    orate the sack of Jerusalem in AD 70.

8. Look at the Roman numerals over the
    entrances to the Colosseum, find an
    example of '4' written IIII, not as IV
    (more common in later Roman times).

9   Sit in the large grassy space which was
    the Circus Maximus and see how many
    kissing couples you can count.

10. Find some tan and black ravens by the
    Tarpeian Rock, the cliff from which they
    threw traitors.

11. Sketch the Pyramid of Cestus, a giant
    Roman tomb outside the oldest city walls.

12. Take a tour of Nero's Golden House, the
    Domus Aurea.

The chariots weren't wooden chariots like the ones in
the film *Ben-Hur*; those were ceremonial chariots, used
for solemn processions. Racing chariots were probably

not much more than a wicker basket on wheels, designed to be as light and fast as possible. Imagine driving a basket on wheels behind four powerful stallions going at breakneck speed. You have the reins wrapped around your waist, to keep your hands free to use the whip or tweak a particular rein. But if you are thrown out of your chariot you will be pulled along the sandy racetrack. Charioteers were given a knife in their belt to cut themselves free of the reins if they were thrown out of the chariot. Imagine trying to cut through eight thick leather straps as you are dragged along the sandy track with horses thundering past on your right and left, their hooves only inches away!

Your tartufo should have arrived by now. As you savour the triple chocolate, remind yourself that chocolate was unknown to the Romans. Poor Romans. But they *did* have chariot races. And we don't. Which would you rather have: chocolate or chariot races?

Now look at some of the Roman men and women walking in the Piazza. Imagine them dressed in tunics and sandals. Imagine the women in stolas and pallas. You can easily see which Roman men would have been patricians or senators. And you can easily spot the rustic farmers and peasants. That beautiful female street-sweeper might have been a slave from Germania. And that muscular youth, showing off to his friends, was probably a gladiator. That man with the thinning hair and the wire-rimmed glasses was an orator, hoping to climb the ladder of honours to the important position of consul. And those street musicians were . . . street musicians!

ROME IN MID-SUMMER

EXCERPTS FROM THE
LIME-COLOURED NOTEBOOK:

THURSDAY 12 JULY 2001 – *Rome*

6.30am – *awake after two maybe three hours of sleep … This is the noisiest hotel room in the world. The sound is amplified by the cobbled streets and stone walls so that it seems LOUDER than if it were right outside. The trucks are as loud as trains, the scooters sound like mosquitoes the size of jet planes. At 4.30am this morning I heard a saucer reverberating as it wobbled on the pavement in ever-decreasing circles, and the sweep of the street cleaner's twig broom as if it was beside my ear. I tried using ear-plugs but the sound was still huge. 'All Rome is at my bed-head' wrote the ancient poet Martial. Now I know what he means!*

7.00am – *The first thing the man at the desk said was 'Your room was noisy? You want to move?' 'Yes.' 'Pack your things and we'll move you to a new room.'*

1.35pm – *Colosseum* – *Women, slaves and poor sat at the very top … special children's section for boys about to make the transition to adulthood and take on the toga praetexta … A man dressed as a legionary crossed the road, mobile phone in one hand, cigarette in the other … postcard with the silhouette of a kitten against the Colosseum.*

2.00pm – *First century fountains! Our guide pointed out little pipes that come out of walls near aqueducts. The water pours out in a steady stream onto a drain in the street below. There is always a little round hole on top of the pipe. If you block the end of the pipe with your*

thumb, the water arcs up out of the hole, like an ancient drinking fountain. Apparently it's safe to drink.
8.45pm – Da Giggetto Restaurant in Rome's Jewish Quarter
…famous fried artichoke here … They bring a platter of fish and you choose the one you want. I choose turbot; it's very flat!

· QUESTION ·

THE KITTEN POSTCARD GAVE ME
AN IDEA FOR THE ASSASSINS OF ROME.
WHO GIVES JONATHAN A KITTEN?

ANSWER: RIZPAH

SEVEN USEFUL ITALIAN PHRASES

I. My name is . . .
    Mi chiamo . . . (mee **kya**-mo)

II. What is your name?
    Come ti chiami? (**ko**-may tee **kya**-mee)

III. Where is the . . .?
    Dov'e il . . .? (doh-**veh** eel . . .?)

IV. I would like that one.
    Vorrei questo. (vor-**ray kwes**-to)

V. I like Roman things.
    Mi piacciono le cose romane (mee pee-ah-
    chun-o lay **co**-say ro-**mah**-nay)

VI. Good bye!
    Arrivederci (ah-ree-veh-**dare**-chee)

VII.Help!
    Aiuto! (eye-**yoo**-doh)

DETECTIVE ASSIGNMENT II: ROME – ANCIENT ROMANS IN THE PIAZZA NAVONA

What you will need: some money and your imagination.

Sit at an outdoor table of the Tre Scalini in Piazza Navona as the afternoon is cooling into evening. Order a tartufo. Tartufo is Italian for truffle. But this is no fungus; it's a triple chocolate ice-cream treat. (You can order something else, if you prefer, but I recommend the tartufo.)

> 'We all have to stay in our lanes until we reach the linea alba, that white line on the track up ahead. And then—' here he tipped his body to the left '—we can try for the inside lane!' He laughed as Nubia screamed again. She had almost fallen out of the little chariot.' (RM XII, p 66)

As you wait for your order to arrive, look at the shape of the Piazza Navona. Does it remind you of anything? It used to be a racecourse for chariots, like the Circus Maximus, only smaller. It was built by the Emperor

Domitian, Titus's younger brother. Where the people are walking and you are sitting used to be the racecourse, with chariots driving at breakneck speed. Imagine four-house chariots driving there now – from your left to your right, and trampling all the unsuspecting tourists!

The central part of the Piazza Navona – with its obelisk and fountains – would have been much thinner in the first century AD, about the width of the base of the obelisk. That was the central barrier of the race-course, called the spina or the euripus. The big fountains wouldn't have been there in Roman times, but parts of the euripus would have been filled with water for the sparsores, the boys who sprinkled the track with water to keep the dust down. Instead of the big fountains at either end, imagine three bronze cones, each about as tall as a cypress tree, set very close together. Those cones were called metae, and they were the turning posts. This is where all the worst crashes occurred, as charioteers made a 180-degree turn at great speed.

POMPEII AND THE BAY OF NAPLES

The Bay of Naples is one of the most beautiful, history-packed places in the world. It is also a very dramatic place. It was here that one of the worst disasters in the history of mankind occurred: the eruption of Vesuvius. A vivid reminder of this is the half-blasted volcano which still looms over the Bay, visible as far south as Sorrento. The city of Pompeii has been extremely well-covered in other guide books and websites, so I am just going to give you a detective assignment and your twelve tasks. Then I'll take you to some of the less visited parts of the Bay of Naples.

But first . . .

CAROLINE'S FIVE TIPS FOR SURVIVING ANCIENT SITES

1. Most countries in the Roman Empire were hot. Make sure you always carry a bottle of water with you to keep hydrated. Have a hat and sunglasses in summer months.

2. Travelling makes me ravenous but when you are in the middle of a Roman site, there is not always a handy food market. So I always carry an apple and a pack of peanuts. Peanuts are my favourite food for staving off hunger pangs for a few hours.

3. If you have a choice, the best time to arrive at popular sites is either just after it opens or late in the day. I like to arrive at Pompeii at around 5.00pm in the afternoon, as the hoards are leaving and the day is cooling off.

4. To avoid disappointment, always check opening times of sites and museums. The tourist office should know.

5. Sometimes the guide book or even the tourist office gets it wrong. Don't be too discouraged if you arrive at a site and find it closed. Relax. Look around for something else to do. It will make a good story when you get home . . . or for your own book!

DETECTIVE ASSIGNMENT III:
EAVESDROPPING IN POMPEII

What you will need: your ears.

Lupus is very good at spying on people and eaves-dropping. In Pompeii you will pass lots of tour groups with different guides speaking in different languages. Choose a guide whose language you understand and try to listen to what they are saying. Pretend to be looking at something else but write down any interesting facts you learn from the guide. Or even from passing tourists.

From a guide at Pompeii, I learned that the fountains were constantly overflowing onto the streets to wash away animal dung and sewage, hence the stepping stones. I also learned about the gladiator-scraping love potion called *gloios* from him.

At Herculaneum, one guide repeated everything at least three times. He was the inspiration for Ascletario in *RM VII.*

> . . . *if you mix some of the gladiator's sweaty scrapings in someone's food then that person will fall in love with you* (RM VI, p 100)

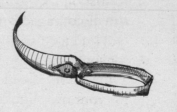

TWELVE TASKS TO DO IN POMPEII (FROM EASY TO CHALLENGING):

1. Find the plaster cast of a dead Roman in the storehouse in the forum.

2. Have your photo taken in the forum with Vesuvius in the background.

3. Look for graffiti on the walls of the Via dell'Abbondanza.

4. Pretend to buy a chickpea pancake from one of the many ancient snack-bars with their sunken holes for amphoras of wine.

5. Locate the fictional site of the blacksmith's shop where Vulcan worked, near the Stabian Gate.

6. Sketch one of the three dog mosaics still in Pompeii (House of the Tragic Poet, House of Proculus Pacuvius, House of the Boar).

7. Touch the place on a fountain where a thousand ancient hands rubbed it smooth.

8. Visit Pompeii's arena and pretend to be either a beast or a beast-fighter.

9. In the gift shop near the cafeteria-restaurant, buy something with CAVE CANEM ('beware of the dog') written on it.

10. Have lunch in the garden restaurant near the gift shop (N.B. You have to pass through the cafeteria to reach it!).

11. Visit the Villa of the Mysteries, outside the Marina Gate past the train station.

12. Go up to the top of Vesuvius and confirm that sulphur smells like rotten eggs.

SERENDIPITY IN SORRENTO –
HOW I FOUND THE VILLA LIMONA

'Let's go on a holiday to Rome and Naples,' said my sister one day, on the phone. I was living in London with my husband Richard, she was raising two boys in California.

'OK,' I said. 'You book the hotel in Rome, and I'll try to find a villa near Pompeii.'

This holiday would be the perfect opportunity to research my next book, which would be set before, during and after the eruption of Vesuvius. I had already decided that Flavia's uncle would own a farm in Stabia, because it's near Pompeii, but not too near.

I phoned a travel firm that specialised in Italian villas.

'I'd like a villa big enough for six people near Stabia,' I said.

Silence. Then 'Do you mean Castellammare di Stabia?' she said. 'We don't have villas there.'

'Or anywhere near Pompeii,' I said. 'I want to be in the plain near Pompeii.'

Another pause. 'Most people stay in Sorrento if they want to visit Pompeii.'

'Do you have villas in Sorrento?'

'Of course.' She went on to describe a big house called the Villa Citrona. Not only was it luxurious, with stunning views, but it had lemon groves and an outdoor swimming pool. And was available for mid-October. The only drawback was that it was up in the hills and we would need to rent a car in Naples. But apart from that, it sounded blissful. The lady asked if I would like to book it.

'Yes,' I said excitedly. 'But I have to ring my sister and confirm it with her. I'll phone you straight back.'

I phoned my sister and told her about the Villa Citrona.

'Sure. Book it,' she said.

I phoned the travel agent. 'I'm sorry,' she said. 'Someone else has just reserved the Villa Citrona. But I can give you the Villa Magnolia, on the Capo di Sorrento.'

'All right,' I sighed, dejected. 'I suppose I'll take that.'

As soon as we arrived in Naples and took the Circumvesuviana train to Sorrento, I realised several things.

First, the area around Pompeii is flat, industrial and ugly. It may have been lush and beautiful in Roman times, but today it's covered with factories and a pall of smog. I'm glad we didn't book a villa in Stabia.

Secondly, it's suicide to rent a car and drive in that part of Italy. Here is a joke the Italians tell: *In Milan, traffic lights are the law. In Rome, traffic lights are a suggestion. In Naples, traffic lights are Christmas decorations.* I'm glad we didn't get the Villa Citrona after all; we would have had to drive everywhere.

Third, being shunted to the Villa Magnolia was one of the best things that could have happened.

The first day we arrived I wandered down to the coast road to explore. I saw a yellow sign – *Ruderi Villa Romana di Pollio Felice 1sec d.C.* – the first century ruins of the Roman Villa of Pollius Felix. I had never heard of any Roman ruins here on the Capo di Sorrento. I followed it down and soon I caught glimpses of the blue sea

35

> The sea blazed like molten copper under the yellow sky of
> dusk and before them, as if floating on the water, was the
> most beautiful villa Flavia had ever seen . . . it had been
> build on an island attached to the mainland by two
> narrow strips of land. . . . There were columns, domes,
> fountains, palm trees and two covered walkways.
> A pool of seawater lay between the villa and the
> mainland, a secret cove, surrounded on all sides by the
> honey-coloured rocks. An arch in the rocks led out to sea,
> making it a small natural harbour. (RM III, p 67)

through the olive trees on my right. Then I came to the
end of the road. Before me lay the headland and the
clear remains of an ancient building. When I saw the
secret cove, I knew this had to be the setting for the
pirates' base in my book.

Back in England I discovered that Pollius Felix had
been a powerful patron – probably of Greek origin –
who lived exactly during the time of Flavia and her
friends. Even more exciting, his wife may have been
Polla Argentaria, the widow of Lucan, a poet who was
implicated in a plot against Nero and forced to kill
himself. A poem by a Roman called Statius describes
Felix's villa and a shrine to Hercules on the Cape of
Surrentum.

Pollius Felix and his wife Polla and their eldest
daughter became some of the most important characters in my books, and two of my favourites in the series
– RM III and RM XI – are set at the Villa of Pollius Felix.
There are still people in the area with the name Pollio

and the beach next to this headland is called Puolo.

If we hadn't ended up at the Villa Magnolia, I might never have learnt of the Villa of Pollius Felix in Sorrento.

By the way, serendipity is when you make an unexpected, lucky discovery.

FLEEING THE VOLCANO

EXCERPTS FROM THE MYRTLEBERRY-COLOURED NOTEBOOK:

FRIDAY 20 OCTOBER 2000 – *Sorrento*

Today's mission: walk around the promontory.

Got up this morning at the crack of dawn to go to the baths and Stabia and some of the lesser known Roman villas, then see if I can walk back around the promontory. On my way down to Sorrento a yellow dog fell into step beside me and kept me company: a modern version of Scuto! I took the train to Castellammare di Stabia where I had a private tour of the opulent Villa Ariadne and Villa San Marco. I was the only one there and was invited to take an early lunch of broccoli leaf sandwiches with some of the archaeologists on the site. They made me try their homemade wine: it was almost black and fizzy. They gave me espresso, too. Now I am going to see if I can retrace the steps of Flavia and her friends when they tried to escape the falling ash of Vesuvius. A nice Italian couple in a shop told me it's about seven kilometres (four miles) to Vico Equense, where I will put my refugee camp.

10.45am – Castellammare di Stabia. There are boatyards, here. Big boats. Navy boats. And handsome naval officers. Fish stalls, too. Selling fish and cockles in flat, round blue tins.

10.50am – Still by the boatyards, I see lots of people crowding around a kind of fountain. Going down some steps to investigate, I see pipes for nine different types of waters: Solfurea Ferrata, Ferrata, Solfurea, Magnesiaca, S. Vincenzo, Media, Acidula, Solfurea Carbonica and Muraglione. I bravely join peasant women and joggers and use my empty water bottle to try the various waters. 'Solfurea' is cold and tastes of eggs: it's sulphur water! The 'Ferrata' is salty and fizzy. The Solfurea Ferrata tastes like fizzy eggs. Both the last two are obviously iron-rich mineral waters ... they leave a rust red deposit at the bottom of my bottle. I wonder if they will turn my tongue red?

> *'You should try the iron water,' said Flavia.*
> *'It turns your tongue red!' (RM III, p 29)*

10.55am – Outskirts of Stabia. I am getting intensely suspicious looks from women hanging out laundry and men on their way to work. But I have made a discovery: if I give them a cheery smile and a bright 'Buon Giorno!', it has the most amazing effect. Immediately the glowering face is transformed to a delighted smile.
11.00am – Just leaving Stabia ... there are some ancient brick arched storage spaces on my left ... old Roman boat houses? Smell of sulphur hits me at the back of the nose, like hard-boiled eggs... It's coming from a trickle of water down the cliff face.
11.10am – 'La Limpida' is the name of a little pebble beach w/ Vesuvius in the background. Only men are swimming here! I think there's a military base nearby.

> *Clio . . . scampered off along the top of the high wall as confidently as if it were a broad pavement. (RM II, p65)*

11.15am – *Walking on the wall around the point of Castellammare because no space on the busy road. I'm Clio!*

11.30am – *Fruit stalls line the busy road beneath the cliffs on my left ... lemons, apples, oranges for sale ... The cliffs are massive, honeycombed with caves. Impossible to convey the size and scale of them.*

Idea: Flavia and her friends will have to come up from the beach onto the road.

Idea for first line!'The mountain had exploded and for three days there was darkness.'

12.00pm a sign:'Welcome to Vico Equense' I made it around the headland!

12.15pm – 'Scraio TERME hotel' Terme means 'baths'... must be nice hot sulphurous baths here ...

12.35pm – Yippee: Vico Equense!

12.45pm – Ahhh! Shade, a cold can of Coke and a rest for my feet. How long did it take me? One hour and forty-five minutes. Walking slowly, taking photos, making notes ...

· QUESTION ·

I GOT THE IDEA FOR THE FIRST LINE FOR ONE OF MY BOOKS WHILE MAKING THIS WALK. WHICH BOOK?

ANSWER: THE PIRATES OF POMPEII

SOME SECRETS OF
THE BAY OF NAPLES

Pompeii is an unmissable site and experience, but it is only one of the many wonders in and around the Bay of Naples. In June of 2005, I was researching the eleventh and most romantic Roman Mystery, which would take place at the Villa of Pollius Felix in Sorrento. In the first century AD, this area was the playground of the rich. I wanted to come here to research my book on Roman decadence, *RM XI*. Richard and I booked a cheap package tour but we also struck off on our own to explore some of the places famous in Roman times.

Here are some of the highlights of our trip.

Our first stop had to be Baia (ancient Baiae) the most notorious of all the towns on the Bay of Naples. It had lots of opulent bathhouses including some where men and women bathed naked together! We first make our way to Pozzuoli – to the west of Naples – via the Circumvesuviana and then by a little SITA bus. There is a Flavian amphitheatre and an entire Roman city in Pozzuoli – now underground – but we will save those for a future visit; I wanted to get to Baia.

After a long wait in the hot sunshine we get a bus to Lago Lucrino. This is the Lucrine Lake, where Nero's mother Agrippina had a villa. One spring evening in AD 65 Nero decided to have her murdered. After his botched plan to drown her in a collapsing boat (she swam ashore), some fishermen picked her up and brought her here, where Nero's assassins finished the job with their swords.

The lake – which was once famous through the Empire for its oysters – is now little more than a stagnant pool, but there is a restaurant on the shore called La Nimphea which overlooks the lake and reminds me of Agrippina's Villa. The train from here to Baia has not run for five years, so we catch another bus. It is only luck that we get out at the right place; the bus driver has no clue where the ancient baths of Baia are. But we spot a brown sign with its white letters, the colour scheme for signs marking ancient sites. A short but exhausting climb up the hill brings us to the entrance. There were many thermal baths here in Baia. A dramatic half dome that we passed on the way up is called the Temple of Diana, but it was actually part of a baths complex.

The site is hot and deserted. We explore the terrace of an opulent villa and the baths surrounding it. We see the odd black and white mosaic, a headless marble statue in a niche, a patch of frescoed wall with traces of expensive 'Egyptian blue' paint. I am hoping to find the so-called Temple of Mercury – a huge dome as big as the Pantheon and pre-dating it – built in the time of Augustus. It was either the apodyterium or frigidarium of this bath complex. I tend to think the latter as it is the outstanding feature of the baths and this is where people would mainly congregate. We go down through ruined porticoes and along a scrubby path fringed with fennel, quince, chamomile, dill, sage and other herbs.

At last we reach a vault which was once one of the rooms of the baths. And here is something I have never seen in my life: a fig tree growing UPSIDE DOWN from the roof of the vault. It is green and healthy and bearing a good crop of figs. What a marvel!

We enter the rectangular room and go through a narrow passage and emerge into another world. Here is a great dome with a circular open skylight at the top and four rectangular openings on its sides. Somehow a breeze is funneled through the openings and caresses us with delicious coolness. The high dome amplifies our whispered exclamations and makes them echo. Sunlight pours almost straight down through the skylight onto four feet of green water – not the original bath, but caused by flooding. The surface of the water, barely rippled by the breeze, throws a huge trembling golden disc back up onto the inner surface of the dome. There are carp swimming in the murky water and a dove flutters above us in the dome. The breeze blows, the water plops, I want to stay in this magical place forever.

Richard and I also make a trip to a village called Piano di Sorrento. In the Museo Georges Vallet there is a beautiful model of the Villa of Pollius Felix.

On mid-summer's day I take the little Roman road down to the villa itself, in order to watch the sun set. The climax of *RM XI* takes place on mid-summer's eve in AD 80. There was a full moon that day and there is another one on midsummer 2005!

On another day we took the Circumvesuviana to the Villa Poppaea at Torre Annunziata, one stop before Pompeii. Archaeologists have been digging in and around Pompeii for at least two hundred years, but this magnificent villa belonging to Nero's wife Poppaea was only unearthed in 1974. We were the only people there except for the usual clutch of site guards relaxing in the shade of a tree. There are columns, frescoes, a wonderful mosaic that looks as if it comes from the 1960s and a huge swimming pool which botanical archaeologists can tell was planted round with oleander and lemon trees. Especially fascinating was looking at the layers of volcanic ash and pumice laid down by Vesuvius opposite the villa.

If you are visiting the Bay of Naples, then a day-trip to Capri is a must. The hydrofoil from Sorrento passes right by the Villa of Pollius Felix, and you can see the three Siren's Islands.

> There were three roughly cube-shaped rocks behind the temple: one medium-sized, the next big and tall and the last very low and flat. (RM XI, p 94)

Although it is high season and Capri is packed with tourists, Richard and I decide to queue up for a boat to the Blue Grotto anyway. What they don't tell you is that once you are at the Blue Grotto it costs another eight and a half euros to get a little rowing boat to take you in. The entrance to the grotto is tiny – hence the rowing boat. Once inside it is cool and echoing and luminously blue, rather like the blue of a swimming pool lit up at night. If you get a chance, visit the ruins of the Emperor Tiberius right up on the highest peak of the island. According to legend Tiberius used to throw unwelcome guests off this cliff. If you are feeling brave you can take a cable car on another part of the island.

For our final day on the Bay of Naples I was determined to try the Roman bath experience. A guide-book mentioned a neoclassical spa built on the ruins of a Roman bath on Ischia, a volcanic island bubbling with hot springs and hot mud. We catch a fast hydrojet from Sorrento to Ischia, and arrive at the baths an hour before their noon closing. While Richard goes off to do a watercolour, I investigate the baths.

A man takes me down to the ancient Roman vaults beneath the modern bath complex. It is very hot and steamy down here. He shows me the hot water bubbling up out of the ground and the hoses that now transfer it up to the baths above us.

Back upstairs in a private cubicle I have a mud bath! You smear slippery grey mud all over your body and they wrap you in a plastic sheet and a cloth sheet. You lie sweating for a quarter of an hour, then they sluice you off and let you soak in a bathtub full of hot mineral water. Finally you can have a massage with lemon-scented cream. In Roman times it would have been scented olive-oil of course, but I imagine the luxurious establishments in Roman Baiae could well have specialised in hot mud treatments.

To celebrate our last evening on the Bay of Naples we go to a five-star hotel in Sorrento called the Bellevue Syrene. I ask to see the Roman rooms downstairs and the nice concierge complies. The replica frescoes and mosaics were done at the beginning of the 20th century and are totally convincing. The setting is magnificent, too. Richard and I have drinks upstairs on the terrace with its Roman-like columns and arbour. I order a non-alcoholic *Sanbitter*; I like it because it's bright red. We sip our drinks and gaze out over the blue Gulf of Sorrento in the cool of the evening. Our cocktails cost as much as dinner but they come with free nibbles and it is worth it for an hour of sybaritic luxury.

TWELVE TASKS TO DO IN THE BAY OF NAPLES (FROM EASY TO CHALLENGING)

1. Sorrento is famous for its lemon groves; try a lemon sorbet or – if your parents are agreeable – get one of them to order *limoncello* after dinner and ask for a sip, but just a sip! It is very strong.

2. Visit Herculaneum and have a photo of yourself taken by a palm tree.

3. Have *Sanbitter* (a bright red, non-sweet, non-alcoholic Italian aperitif) and nibbles on the terrace of the Hotel Bellevue Syrene in Sorrento; ask if you can see the Roman rooms first.

4. Sketch the fighting cockerels mosaic at the National Museum of Archaeology in Naples.

5. Visit the amazing Villa of Poppaea (one stop away from Pompeii at Torre el Greco) and look at the cake-like layers of ash and pumice that Vesuvius laid down.

6. Find one of the public water spouts in Stabia and taste the mineral water.

7. Go all the way into the Blue Grotto in Capri.

8. Visit the model of the Villa of Pollius Felix in Piano di Sorrento.

9. Swim in the secret cove of the Villa of Pollius Felix on the Capo di Sorrento.

10. Find the little fresco of Perseus with the head of Medusa at the Villa San Marco at Castellammare di Stabia.

11. Have your photo taken beside the upside-down fig tree next to the so-called Temple of Mercury at Baia (don't forget to go into the flooded and domed room next door).

12. Take a hot mud bath in a spa on the island of Ischia.

GREECE

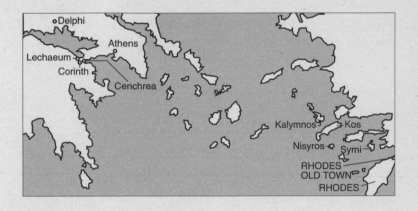

GREECE

Richard and I made several trips to Greece to research books IX and X: *The Colossus of Rhodes* and *The Fugitive from Corinth*.

RHODES AND THE GREEK ISLANDS

There are many Greek islands, but when I was researching *RM IX*, Richard and I visited some called the Dodecanese off the southwest coast of Turkey. 'Dodekanesa' is Greek for twelve islands. There are actually about twelve big islands and over a hundred smaller ones. Rhodes is the biggest of the twelve. We also visited Symi, Kalymnos, Kos and Nisyros, a volcanic island. I was particularly interested in Symi, which is Lupus's birthplace and in Rhodes, where some important scenes in the book would take place.

For our first trip, in the spring of 2003, we flew from London to Rhodes and we spent our first night in a room built into the wall of Rhodes Old Town. We then took a ferry to the island of Kalymnos where we spent ten days in the little village of Myrties, hosted by an English couple who lived in a tiny shepherd's cottage on a hillside. Faith Warn has written a book called *Bitter Sea* about sponge divers and I first met her while I was researching *RM V*. Faith and her husband Al met us off the ferry from Rhodes, took us to a little apartment which they had booked for us, fed us and drove us around. They even took us to the house of some Greek friends for a memorable Easter lunch. (I dedicated *RM IX* to Faith and Al for their *philoxenia*: hospitality.)

When we got back to Rhodes, we spent our last four days at one of the most magical places I have ever been to: Marco Polo Mansions in Rhodes Old Town. The hotel – an old Venetian mansion – is a work of art: sculpted plaster arches and stairs painted raspberry red, lemon yellow, sapphire blue and terracotta. All the rooms are grouped around a garden courtyard full of green plants and fragrant flowers, just like a Roman villa. Each of the rooms is unique and one even has its own mini hammam instead of a conventional bath-room. The owners are Effi – a Kalymniot fluent in English and Italian – and her husband Spiro.

One day we took a boat to the island of Symi, one of the standard day-trips out of Rhodes. Symi is Lupus's home and I wanted to make sure I saw where he was born.

TWELVE TASKS TO DO IN THE GREEK ISLANDS (FROM EASY TO CHALLENGING):

1. Train yourself to say 'no' by tipping your head backwards, in the Greek style.

2. Learn the Greek alphabet and have a go at reading Greek signs.

3. Buy one of those blue glass eyes that turns away evil; you can find them everywhere, especially on worry-beads and key-chains.

4. Identify a myrtle bush and pick one leaf. Crush it and smell it.

5. Buy a sea sponge and try washing yourself with it that night in the bath.

6. Go to a Greek market and bargain for something a Roman might have used.

7. Try a sip of retsina (resin-flavoured wine) from a copper beaker.

8. Leave a little offering at a roadside shrine, or light a candle in a chapel.

9. Buy a goat bell (try an ironmonger's shop).

10. Sketch an interesting-looking person.

11. Fill your water bottle from a fountain.

12. Buy mastic resin and chew it; or try a sip of 'mastiha' (an ouzo–like aperitif but flavoured with mastic instead of aniseed).

Young man w/ very dark hair & smooth skin. Doesn't look Kalymnian! Upward slanting eyes straight eyebrows Hair smooth until pony- tail when it all turns curly!

2/5/03 10:45 pm Rembetika

EASTER ON KALYMNOS

EXCERPTS FROM THE
CHERRY-COLOURED NOTEBOOK:

WEDNESDAY 23 APRIL 2003 – *arrival in Rhodes Old Town*
Grey sky, breezy, but not too cold … We are staying in Cava D'Oro, a
hotel built into the thick town wall, just as Flavia's house is built into
the wall of Ostia!
The shops here in the Old Town are just like shops in Ostia: deep but
narrow, having shop fronts w/ shutters. They even sell the same types
of goods: cloth and tapestry, copper, leather, souvenirs, pottery, glass,
jewellery, shoes and sandals … The blue eye good-luck charm is
everywhere: on key-chains, worry beads, earrings, pendants …
The blue eye is apotropaic: it turns away bad luck.

THURSDAY 24 APRIL 2003
Our ferry arrived in Kalymnos after dark but Al and Faith were
there waiting! They gave us cheery waves, helped us pile our luggage
into their car, drove us to their village: Myrties. It means 'myrtle'
which is nice: Captain Geminus's ship was the Myrtilla, named after
Flavia's mother, who was named after the myrtle bush. We had
dinner on their balcony and Al cooked a delicious Greek dish called
gigantes. It is broad beans and sausage in a thyme-scented tomato
sauce. They served it with choriatiki – Greek peasant salad – and
cold retsina.

FRIDAY 25 APRIL 2003 – *Myrties, Kalymnos*
8.20am – Going for an early morning walk … the musky acrid scent

of a fox as I climb a steep road up to a little church. The sea goes from jade green at the shore to cobalt blue with almost no grading ... The clang of a church bell. Rather flat and perfunctory, like the clang of the gong announcing opening of baths? Now I can hear the distant tinkle of goat bells ... Later I get on a bus and am greeted with a joyful 'Kali anastasi! Have a good Resurrection time!' After Saturday midnight they say 'Christos anesti!' (Christ is risen) and you reply: 'Alithos anesti!' (He is risen indeed.)

SATURDAY 26 APRIL 2003 – *Myrties*
9.50am – A sparkling, blustery morning ... Today is the day they prepare the sheep. As I was walking back I saw a Toyota pick-up with three very subdued sheep riding in the back... I wonder if they knew where they were going?
11.45am – On our way into Pothias we see them burning an effigy of Judas; this reminds me of Guy Fawkes ...
Later we watch the Greek family prepare a goat and put the whole thing in a big tin box. There are three daughters in this family and each one puts a tinned goat into the domed clay outdoor oven. They seal the door of the oven with mud. One of the rituals is that they try to daub each other's faces with this mud. Much laughter and shouting ... The oven reminds me of Jesus's tomb: is this intentional? Almost every house in Kalymnos has one of these domed outdoor ovens ...
That night there is a big procession in Pothia with elaborate floats ... Whole families are there, from tiny babies to ancient grandmothers and even TEENAGE BOYS AND GIRLS! Afterwards men throw dynamite from the hills either side so the bangs echo back and forth ... They pronounce it dee-na-MEE-tayz. They love their dee-na-MEE-tayz here on Kalymnos. Faith and Al tell us that the dynamite-throwers often lose fingers or hands. One year two young men killed

GREECE

themselves. Later, back in our village, there is midnight mass. When it's over, everyone will go to eat meat. (They've been fasting from meat for forty days.)

SUNDAY 27 APRIL 2003 – *Easter morning, Kalymnos*
On my morning walk, I saw a man 'unsealing' the 'tomb' of his oven by picking the dried mud off. Later, when I passed by again on my way home, the oven was unsealed but not open.

The family invites us to share lunch. This big extended family sits around a long table in the courtyard of their houses. The tradition in Kalymnos is that the father gives each daughter her own house on the day of her wedding. This family is rich and the father built each of his four daughters houses near his. One daughter died recently and they plan to erect a little chapel to her right here in the compound. The children run around, the women prepare food, and the black-sheep of an uncle arrives and tells tall tales of his wayward youth.

After lunch we all go to the waterfront of Pothia to enjoy the spring sunshine at outdoor cafés. Even though Christ has risen, people are still throwing exploding caps on the ground and the sound of dynamite rings in the natural amphitheatre of this port town.
Faith told me the order of events:
Good Friday evening: the procession with floats of Christ's tomb
Saturday afternoon: dynamite, burning the effigy of Judas and preparing the lamb or goat for the oven
Saturday night: Midnight mass followed by a meal
Sunday lunchtime: eating the lamb or goat
Sunday evening: dynamite and dancing

MONDAY 28 APRIL 2003 – *Easter Monday, Telendos Island*
Faith and Al have taken us across the strait to have a picnic on the little
island of Telendos … Apparently it used to be part of the mainland, but
five hundred years ago an earthquake separated it and made it an
island … There are no roads here and only one guest-house … We sit
on the shore under tamarisk trees on a bed of papery dried seaweed
and eat feta cheese, from Faith and Al's shepherd landlord, choriatiki
made by Faith, and coarse brown bread. We wash it down w/ retsina,
the famous Greek white wine that tastes of pine resin. It is utterly
silent. I can hear a raven or crow's harsh cry on the left, cheeping
of birds on right, lap of water (no waves), a cockerel crowing across
the water …

TUESDAY 29 APRIL 2003 – *Kalymnos*
Faith and Al take us to the Cave of St Panteleimon, a saint who heals …
Under the saint's icon I see tin votive relief plaques which people have
left: a pair of eyes, leg, arm, a baby, a woman in a 1950s type skirt (for
marriage apparently), a house, an ear, a boy in short trousers … You
can buy these at the chapel nearby …

WEDNESDAY 30 APRIL 2003 – *Kalymnos Folklore Museum*
In olden times, Kalymniots dipped their finger in a dish of rock salt
and cloves, then used finger to brush their teeth … they played games
with knucklebones, nuts, pebbles, marbles … if a young woman wore a
headscarf with the eagle showing, that meant she was single … girls
married as young as twelve, but sixteen was the usual age … on the
first day a baby was born he was washed in warm sea water to get
him used to the sea … on the third day after a birth, three sweet
pastries were left out for the Three Fates, so that they would be kind
to the baby …

MAY DAY! THURSDAY 1 MAY 2003

Went to fill bottle with water from the spring, like a good Greek girl …
Today you put a wreath of flowers on your front door. Or on the front
of your car! On the way back from the spring I saw a local woman
gathering wildflowers, so I did, too. Red poppies, yellow daisies, white
chamomile, purple trumpets and pink morning glory … I made a little
bouquet and tied it to the front door with a white ribbon taken from
one of the tin votives. Does this custom date back to ancient times?
It must.

Later, I decide to walk to Pothia, a few miles away.

8.20am – A lamb with a black and white face says 'baaaa?' but as a
question. I've never heard such a human-sounding animal.

8.35am – A vase with silk flowers by the roadside and an icon of Mary
nailed to a pine tree …

8.50am – Another shrine by the road; silk flowers and real chamomile
in a glass jar (knocked over) and an icon of Christ.

9.00am – I've arrived at the graveyard of Chora. Almost all the graves
are white marble, most with fresh flowers or colourful plastic wreathes.
Some with little glass cases under the cross. In these cases: portrait photo
of the deceased, icons, flowers, candles, glass goblets, tiny hurricane
lamps, crystal crosses, Barbie doll-sized ceramic statues of Christ …
pictures of the whole family … a lamp is burning: someone has been
here to tend it. A man comes to a grave, crosses himself and begins to
address the tombstone in a low voice.

9.45am – Outskirts of Pothia. Up on the hill I can see the church of St
Savas …

10.00am – There is a niche-shrine in the wall and the pavement is
very high, like Pompeii. Faith says when it rains the streets become
torrents …

*10.55am – Backstreets of Pothia … A tiny hole-in-the-wall bakery.
Baker is using a long flat shovel thing to remove the bread. Just like
Roman times!*

FRIDAY 2 MAY 2003 – *Pothia, the port of Kalymnos*
*12.30am – At a Rembetika Tavern, waiting for the 3.00am Ferry back
to Rhodes.*
*Faith, Al, Richard and I had a late dinner here listening to musicians
play rembetika, a kind of folk music. Now it's after midnight but they
are still singing …*
3.20am – On ferry – Faith and Al stayed to wave us off!

· QUESTION ·

I AM INTRIGUED BY THE IDEA OF
CHARMS WHICH TURN AWAY EVIL. AT
THE BEGINNING OF RM IX, WHO GIVES
THE FOUR FRIENDS SUCH
APOTROPAIC CHARMS?

ANSWER: ALMA

DETECTIVE ASSIGNMENT IV:
FAITH AND SUPERSTITION
IN THE GREEK ISLANDS

What you will need: sharp eyes, good observing powers and an open mind.

The Greeks and Romans worshipped many gods who each had different functions. For example Asklepios (or Aesculapius) was a god of healing. Christians often built churches on the sites of temples and assigned shrines to a saint, like Saint Panteleimon in Kalymnos. If you look carefully you can often see the pagan origins of Christian buildings or customs. Look for the following and tick them when you find them:

- someone making a sign against evil (e.g. crossing oneself, knocking on wood, etc.)

- a votive plaque or other object offered in fulfilment of a vow, or as a reminder of a prayer

- a statue of a god, goddess or saint

- a niche in walls or street corners

- a shrine by the sides of roads

- an apotropaic amulet (good luck charm) on trucks, cars, cart or someone's neck

- a modern animal sacrifice (like slaughtering a sheep or goat)

- a religious practice (like throwing dynamite or burning an effigy of Judas)

- a modern tomb or a grave

- someone dressed as a religious figure

- an ancient Roman or Greek altar

- any other remnant of ancient worship or superstition

MORE EXCERPTS FROM THE
CHERRY-COLOURED NOTEBOOK:

SATURDAY 3 MAY 2003 – *Marco Polo Mansions, Rhodes Old Town*

1.15pm – *Tired after our late-night ferry ... having a siesta in our mustard-yellow room. It's very dim and a breeze brings the cheerful sound of Greeks arguing. Our barred window looks directly out onto one of the Old Town's narrow cobbled back streets. People walk past only six feet away – with no idea that I can hear every word ... Through the open doorway the inner garden is very bright ... palm fronds, blue sky, ivy leaves on trellis ... Sound of birds cheeping sleepily, piercing cries of swifts, the ubiquitous cockcrow, and wind chimes! As soon as you step into the town square you hear the wind chimes tinkling ... I can smell damp plaster, and the faint remnant of anti-mosquito incense. No motorized vehicles are allowed in Rhodes Old Town, so traffic is a very dim low rushing sound occasionally overlaid with the sound of a scooter: they are allowed!*

SUNDAY 4 MAY 2003 – *Rhodes Old Town*

6.00pm – *We are having dinner at a little taverna in Rhodes Old Town. It's called Mystagogia. A 'mystagogue' is someone who shows you secret things ... The owner, Philip, serves tsadziki (yogurt flavoured with dill and garlic) on a round dish, made to look like a face! Cucumber ears, dill weed for hair, sweet pepper mouth and two black olive eyes! For dessert he serves slices of sweet red apple on thick Greek yogurt, then drizzled all over with honey. This could be one of Alma's desserts!*

It's hard to get used to the head signal for 'no'. The head goes back. For 'yes', an inclination to the side.

MONDAY 5 MAY 2003
9.25am – On the Symi II: a one-day excursion to Symi from Rhodes
10.07am – Approaching Symi
On our right is a long narrow spur of Turkish coast like a Lizard's Tail. It would surely have been a landmark Lupus and all Symiots would have known.
11.15am – Looking for dolphins but can't see any. Faith and Al told us that after one particularly bad storm there were a lot of dead jellyfish floating on the water: a carpet of jellyfish.

> 'I've never seen so many before.'
> She looked down at the hundreds
> of grey blobs floating in the
> harbour water. . . . When
> Zosiumus saw the undulating
> carpet of jellyfish his eyes grew
> wide. (RM IX, p 128)

12.40pm – Gialos, the harbour town of Symi! Houses buttermilk and red rise up the hillside, spikes of dark cypress trees rising among them …
1.10pm – At Taverna Meraklis (recommended by Faith and Al) Symi shrimp, small and sweet, not too fishy – Nubia might say: 'They taste pink!'

2.30pm – I have found the site of Lupus's house. It is a little mini cove around the corner from the boatyard. Now known as PARADEISOS (in Greek of course) or 'Paradise Symi'. A gravel beach, blue water, lots of ancient tamarisks, grey and apricot-coloured rocks ...

3.00pm – The church here above Lupus's house would have been a temple in Roman times ... Pines, oleanders, thistles, black and white pebble mosaic ... I can smell donkey dung ...

3.40pm – On the Symi II ready to go back to Rhodes ... I found everything I had to – especially the site of Lupus's house!

· QUESTION ·

I LIKED THE IDEA OF A MYSTAGOGUE,
SOMEONE WHO SHOWS YOU SECRET
THINGS. IN WHICH OF MY BOOKS DO I
HAVE A CHARACTER CALLED
MYSTAGOGUS?

ANSWER: THE FUGITIVE FROM CORINTH

DETECTIVE ASSIGNMENT V:
ANCIENT FOOD

What you will need: your courage.

Food is always a good way to go back to Roman times, or at least to get you thinking about it. When many people travel, their first experience of food while travelling is the hotel breakfast. Some hotels just offer stale croissants and sweetened juice. Others offer tables groaning with a huge selection of food. Don't go straight for you usual cornflakes and orange juice. Try something else. Try cheese, bread and olives – a plausible Roman breakfast. Or some local porridge, another likely breakfast. Be as brave as you dare in trying out new foods. Here are some of the foods you might be presented with in Greece. Tick them off if you have even one tiny bite:

- shrimp
- goat
- lamb or mutton (sheep)
- olives
- dolmades (grape leaves stuffed with rice and pine nuts)
- kalamari (little squid)
- gigantes (butter beans in a tomato herb sauce)
- choriatiki (Greek peasant salad with cucumber and raw onion)
- tsadziki (yogurt with garlic and dill)
- pitta bread (flat bread like some found at Pompeii)
- hummus (chickpea paste with tahina, garlic and lemon juice)

- spanakopita (spinach and filo pastry pie)
- tyropita (cheese and filo pastry pie)
- moussaka (dish with aubergine, potato, tomato and lamb mince)
- feta cheese
- pistachio nuts
- baklava (pastry made with nuts and honey)

Your parents might try ouzo (aniseed/liquorice-flavoured aperitif), mastiha (mastic-flavoured aperitif) or the popular resin-flavoured wine called retsina. It was probably very similar to Roman wine because Romans lined their wine amphoras with pine pitch.

As you eat, consider whether Flavia and her friends might have known these foods. Some foods the Romans didn't know about were tomatoes, chocolate, vanilla, potatoes, pineapples, bananas, coffee or tea. Can you think of any others?

ATHENS

Although Athens was the greatest city of Greece's Golden age, by Flavia's time (the first century AD) it was just a small university town. At that time, Corinth was the most important city on mainland Greece.

Still, I thought Flavia and her friends should visit the home of Socrates, Plato and Xenophon, so I brought them to Athens in my tenth book, *RM X*.

I will never forget my first trip to Greece. I was a student at Cambridge and had been studying Classics for four years. As the plane banked over Athens I was so excited. I have three outstanding memories from that first trip:

1. The Agora Museum, in the brilliantly reconstructed Stoa of Attalos.
2. Smelling wisteria for the first time. I stood under a blooming arbour of it in the National Gardens in Athens and practically swooned from the honey-sweet scent.
3. Going for a meal in the Plaka district near the Acropolis and watching a waiter break plates in time to bouzouki music.

ATHENS IN DECEMBER

EXCERPTS FROM THE LAVENDER-COLOURED NOTEBOOK:

THURSDAY 23 DECEMBER 2004 – *Athens*

1.00pm – *Climbing from Athenian agora to the acropolis, a steep climb …shaggy pines and prickly pines, olive trees …*

1.05pm – *Amazing boulders between Acropolis and Areopagus, the hillside here is perfect for caves …*

1.40pm – *Real sense of the dramatic approaching the Doric columns of the Propylea*

1.45pm – *I've just bought a brilliant map of the ancient acropolis precinct …*

2.20pm – *The acropolis is stupendous, even covered with scaffolding. We are practically the only ones here …*

2.45pm – *On our way out, by the little Temple of Athena Nike near the Propylea … there seems to be a sheer drop over the side of the acropolis, but when you peer over, you see it's only a short hop down!*

FRIDAY 24 DECEMBER – *Christmas Eve, Athens*

8.00am – *a cold clear morning on Lycabettus. Santa Claus is walking down the road!*

DELPHI AND CORINTH

'It never rains in Delphi,' said our guide, 'It's Apollo there: the god of light.'

When we arrived in Delphi it was raining. But it soon cleared up and the site was left as slick and polished as a jewel. I am surprised by how steeply the sanctuary of Delphi rises up its green mountain, even though I have read about it many times. Clouds still drift in the sky and I have a sudden image of the colossal statue of Apollo with his head swallowed by cloud. This gives me another idea: maybe it is the first time Nubia has ever been 'in a cloud'.

> 'Clouds are like fog,' said Nubia
> over her shoulder as they emerged
> from a cloud and began the descent
> to Delphi. 'Just fog.'
> (RM X, p 103)

69

Today there is almost nothing to mark the two great harbours of Corinth in her heyday, when she was the richest city in Greece. In the first century AD they were teeming with activity, colour, noise. Today there are just a few columns, some clay roof tiles and maybe a partially preserved mosaic. Nobody comes here. Our Athenian taxi driver Stavros – born and bred just a few miles away – had never been to either site and had a job finding them.

First we visited the site of Lechaeum, the western harbour on the Isthmus of Corinth. Somehow I felt that Lechaeum should be more industrial and Cenchrea – the eastern harbour – more luxurious. I'm not sure why. Perhaps facts I've read and then forgotten, perhaps intuition. Perhaps a combination of the two. But when I visited Lechaeum, I was surprised by how much it resembled my mental picture of it. Rather bleak, flat, scrubby ground covered with dried grasses and gorse, and a shingle beach rather than a sandy one.

Waves hiss up in short little gasps. The acrocorinth looms behind. I can imagine slaves unloading the ships and their cries as they pull the empty hull up onto its cart to transport it along a track called the diolkos over four miles of dry barren stony land. Here in Lechaeum the water is a flat pewter colour, lit by shafts of silver light from a hazy sun. Up on the Acrocorinth you might be able to hear the clanking goat bells, bees buzzing, the wind sighing and – far off in the valley – a donkey's wheezing bray.

Half an hour later, at the eastern harbour of Cenchrea, the sea is sapphire blue beneath a warm, golden sun. That part of the coast is lush and luxurious, with dramatic mountains ending in blue water. There are olive groves, vines and scented bushy pine trees that are bright green rather than dark green. I even find the spring which pours from the coast into the sea and terracotta flues that prove the Romans had indeed built a baths complex here. This is called Loutro Heleni, which means 'Helen's Baths'. This gives me an idea for the name of the owner of the hospitium where Flavia's father always stays when he takes his ship across the isthmus.

On the way back to Athens, Stavros tells us his favourite restaurant. It is called Fagopoteion – which roughly means 'Food and Drink' – and it's wonderful. It's full of Athenians – a good sign – and you can just point to the food you want. For the first time we see the wine being drawn from a barrel into copper beakers. We've used up almost all our money but when I ask the owner if he takes cards he says, 'You don't need cards. We're very cheap.' And indeed they are. Although the restaurant is in the upmarket Kolonaki district of Athens, the whole meal with wine costs only twenty euros and it's one of the best we had.

TWELVE TASKS TO DO IN AND AROUND ATHENS (FROM EASY TO CHALLENGING):

1. Learn how to say say 'hello', 'please', 'thank you' and 'toilets?' in Greek.
2. Sketch the magnificent boy on a horse sculpture in the National Museum of Athens.
3. Find a statue with traces of paint on it in the new Acropolis Museum.
4. Climb up to the top of the Areopagus.
5. Go to the National Gardens and sniff some plants which the ancient Greeks and Romans would have known.
6. Listen to bouzouki music in a taverna on the Plaka.
7. Go to the wonderful Agora Museum with its reconstructed Stoa of Attalos and find a ceramic baby's potty.
8. Visit the tower of the Winds in the Roman Agora.
9. In Delphi, touch the replica omphalos or navel of the world.
10. In Delphi, find the famous bronze statue called the Charioteer of Delphi.
11. Go up to the top of the Acrocorinth and list five different noises you can hear.
12. Find Helen's Bath in Cenchrea and feel the temperature of the water.

DETECTIVE ASSIGNMENT VI: OBSERVING AND DESCRIBING A PERSON

What you will need: a friend or family member.

Find a table or somewhere to sit where you can observe people. Have your partner facing you, so they can see over your shoulder. Turn around and find someone. A fisherman mending his nets. Or a woman walking her dog. Or a couple at another table. Very quickly look them up and down. Now turn back to your friend and describe the person.

Tell your helper the basics first: hair colour and clothing. See if you can guess at height, weight and age. Then see if you can recall quirks or other distinguishing marks. What nationality are they? (Waiters are very good at telling someone's nationality based only on their appearance.)

As you describe the person your friend says yes or no. They are looking at the person and can help you remember. After some practice you will get much better at this. Good detectives and good writers must be observant.

NORTH AFRICA

NORTH AFRICA

I had always wanted to visit North Africa and a good excuse was to set some books there! The Roman Mysteries set in North Africa are books *XIV* and *RM XV*: *The Beggar of Volubilis* and *The Scribes from Alexandria*.

MOROCCO

Of all the places I have visited, Morocco is the most like ancient Rome. You can still shop in narrow cobbled streets of a walled town without traffic, where donkeys and horses are the transportation. You can go to a hammam, the closest thing to the Roman baths. You can choose a live chicken for your dinner and watch the chicken seller kill it, pluck it and gut it before your eyes. You can watch tanners, carpet-weavers, copper-beaters and mosaic-cutters at work. You can barter in a covered souk for copper bangles, silk tassels or wooden bowls.

Richard and I went to Morocco in the first few days of 2006 to research my fourteenth book, *RM XIV*. We visited the Roman ruins of Volubilis and Lixus, the archaeological museum at Rabat, a bird sanctuary lagoon and the wonderful Djema el Fna Square in Marrakech, with its snake charmers, soup sellers and dentists. But three experiences in particular transported me back to Roman times: a hammam, a souk and the slaughter of a ram.

*

It was warm the night we arrived in Marrakech but soon after we see Volubilis, the weather grows cold and wet. The train to Fes doesn't help. It is an ancient unheated creature whose windows are so misted that we can barely see the countryside. The train arrives in Fes late in the afternoon. We catch a taxi to the Hotel Batha (pronounced Bat-ha) and turn on the heating. Soon the room will be warm. Meanwhile, one of my guide books says there is a hammam near here and as I haven't done anything for research purposes that day, I decide to be brave and go. I pack a towel, shampoo, soap, face cream, a hairbrush and a spare pair of underpants. Stepping outside the hotel, I find it still raining, and dark now, too. A peanut-seller kindly shows me to the unmarked door of the hammam and beams a toothless smile. I tip him a couple of dirham. In the entryway I buy a ticket from an old man. Entry to the hammam costs eighteen dirham, about one pound fifty.

I pass through ancient double wooden doors to find a steamy, marble-floored room with a fountain at its centre and a gutter and on three sides a low stone balcony with women changing. Just like a Roman apodyterium. I give my ticket to the lady, rent a 'locker' (wooden box above the bench) and agree to a massage for fifty dirham, about four pounds. I undress like everyone else, and put my clothes in the niche overhead. An old lady grips me with a calloused hand and pulls me across the slippery floor to a room around a corner. This room is laid out just like several Roman baths whose ruins I've seen: marble-veneer floor, ceramic-tiled walls, high vaulted ceiling and two deep square stone basins, one for very hot water, one for cold water. There are naked women

Bronze horse and jockey
National Museum, Athens, Greece – see p 67, 72

Upside down fig tree
Baia, Italy – see p 41

The so-called 'Temple of Diana'
Baia, near Naples, Italy – see p 41

Shrine on the evil stairs
Coastal road from Corinth to Athens, Greece – see p 67-71

Fisherman on the Nile
Near Luxor, Egypt – see p 99, 104

Roman Theatre
Sabratha, Italy – see p 13

The Stoa of Attalos
Athens, Greece – see p 72

Banks of the Nile
Near Esna, Egypt – see p 99

Fresco from the Villa Poppaea
Torre Annunziata, near Pompeii, Italy – see p 42

Richard and Caroline at the Temple of Luxor
Luxor, Egypt – see p 99

Village market
Souk El Arba, Morocco – see p 79

Covered souk
Marrakech, Morocco – see p 79

S. S. Karim steamboat
Luxor, Egypt – see p 99, 104

Sage tea
Berber village near Marrakech, Morocco – see p 84

Caroline at the Villa Poppaea
Torre Annunziata, near Pompeii, Italy – see p 42

Caroline with her notebooks

everywhere, sitting on the stone floor surrounded by buckets. These buckets are plastic, but would have been wood or leather in Roman times. There are females of all ages here, from little girls to old women. They are washing their bodies, their hair, even their clothes. Like some Roman baths, this one has certain hours for women and certain hours for men. This means the bathhouse is quite nice, too. I later went to a hammam in Marrakech which had separate facilities for men and women. The men had the nicer downstairs facility; the women had a Spartan upstairs room. No decorations, no big basins, just a tile floor and pipes with taps coming out of the wall.

Anyway, back in the Fes hammam, my old lady guide takes me into a second steam room, almost identical to the first but less crowded. She gets me to sit on the hot, wet stone floor and starts tipping buckets of deliciously warm water over me. Then she asks for my shampoo and when I produce a bottle, she washes my hair, brushes it through and rinses it with a bucket. Bliss. Now another lady with a red bandana type headscarf takes a scrubbing glove and rubs me hard all over. She uses a soap made of olive oil. It is like black butter. The scrubbing is almost painful, probably because I'm not used to it. I am lying on my back. The floor is heated underneath in Roman style and almost burns my toes; I remember that ancient Romans used to wear wooden bath clogs.

I close my eyes and try to relax. Before she gets me to turn onto my front she shows me the worms of grey skin she has rubbed off me. Eww. After she scrubs my back they sluice me off. Then a third headscarfed lady gives me my massage, rubbing me painfully hard with my bar of soap. Finally, they sluice me down with gaspingly cold water, and wander off to find their next victim.

Time is passing, so I stand up and hurry back through the two steamy rooms to my locker in the apodyterium and start to dry myself. Suddenly I feel a bit sick. I have to put my head between my knees. It occurs to me that I should have rested after the bath. That's what a Roman would have done. Eventually I feel well enough to get dressed and go back to the hotel. I feel clean, relaxed and soft. And for the first time in days, I am warm!

The next day we meet our guide for the day, Ali, the relative of a man we met on the train. Ali is dressed in the 'uniform' of Morocco, a djellaba with a hood. There is something sinister about his pointy hood but he seems very nice. Ali has a car and speaks good English. He drives us past the golden walls of the Medina to a ceramics factory. The potteries used to be inside the city walls, but the olive pits which fuel the kilns caused so much billowing black smoke that they had to move. There are very few people around neither tourists nor workers. The mosaic-cutters' room is like stepping back in time. The men and boys squat round low tables in a plaster-walled room and chip away at the ceramic tiles, making stars, hexagons, diamonds and all the other shapes that make up the mosaic walls, columns and fountains you see everywhere. Next we visit the back of the factory where there are six big circular pits in the ground. This is where clay from the mountains is soaked and kneaded (by bare foot) to make it soft enough to work. The ground is slippery here from yesterday's heavy rainfall. We see the kiln being fired, get a demonstration of a foot-powered potter's wheel and see the glazing room. Nothing can have changed in two thousand years.

We leave the pottery and Ali drives us to a parking space outside the Medina walls. No traffic is allowed inside, and all goods are carried on donkey, mule or horseback. Ali was born and raised here in the Fes medina; he often stops to greet friends and we are never pestered.

First he takes us to the famous tanneries. You go up narrow stairs through a leather-goods shop to a high balcony where you can look down over them. Another guide offers us a mint-tea and as we sip it he explains how things work. The raised pits are for tanning and dyeing the leather. The hay-strewn flat rooftops for drying, the running water for washing. The guide gives us a piece of mint to put under our noses. If the stench of the lye, dye and pigeon dung used to treat the skins is this bad mid-winter, think how terrible it will be in the heat of the summer.

Next Ali leads us through narrow winding streets past mosaic-covered mosques and fountains. Every so often we have to flatten ourselves against a wall to allow a donkey to pass. I see a young man feeding sawdust to the underground furnace of a hammam, just like a slave in Roman times would have fuelled a hypocaust. We don't buy a carpet at the six-hundred-year-old carpet shop and we don't even go into the jeweller's or embroiderer's. But we do let Ali take us to the apothecary. This is a narrow Aladdin's cave of coloured powders and dried lizards and bottles of oil. We sniff lots of perfumes and aromatic spices and Richard buys half a pound of cumin and 'Moroccan curry powder' to experiment with at home. I buy a textured glove and some black butter soap for my next hammam.

Finally we have lunch on a padded divan with a table before us. I am tempted to recline as they bring saucers of Moroccan delicacies. I can imagine Alma preparing dishes like these: carrots with cumin, chopped cabbage and turnip, cauliflower with spices, olives, hummus, tsadziki, spiced lentils, chicken with apricot and sweet mint tea to finish.

For our last day in Morocco we are back in Marrakech, staying at a delightful hotel with tiled courtyards called the Hotel Gallia. Our flight back to London is not until the evening so we have all day. The hotel staff find a Berber driver to take us into the hills near Marrakech and show us some villages. Our guide's name is Mohammed and he tells us that today is a Muslim Festival called the Day of the Sheep. Three million rams will have their throats cut all over Morocco and everyone is at home. It's the equivalent of Christmas, or the Saturnalia. I feel bad that Mohammed is not spending time with his family. He says we are welcome to come to his mother's house where they will be killing a ram at 11.00am. We say yes. How often do you get to visit a home of one of the locals? Mohammed drives us through a deserted Marrakech and out onto the plain. He explains that he is a Valley Berber. His village is about forty-five minutes drive from Marrakech. It is constructed of bricks and the red earth found all over this part of Morocco.

Mohammed's mother's house is built around a courtyard with a small square of garden in the middle. Giving onto this courtyard is the entryway – just like a Roman vestibule – a dining room, a kitchen, bedroom and also an enclosure for farm animals with a tiny domed two-person hammam inside. In a niche in the only wall of the courtyard is a hand pump to bring water from the well. Electricity was installed only three years ago; until then they lived by candlelight.

Mohammed's sister greets us with a basket of cookies, some are shaped like stars and some shaped like Christmas trees. We sit in the sunny courtyard at a plastic table and Mohammed's young wife serves us sweet sage tea, the preferred winter drink. Her hands are decorated with a complicated henna design. She is wearing a bathrobe as a coat because although it's sunny, it's a cool day. Presently the village elder arrives along with Mohammed's brother and they drag a reluctant ram from the animal enclosure out of the house to a patch of waste ground by a thorn hedge. The elder faces east and says a prayer. Then as Mohammed and his brother hold the ram down he cuts its throat. It takes the ram a good few minutes to die, the last minute spent scrabbling in the dust, desperately fighting death. The blood is startlingly vivid. I have been eating meat all my life, but this is the first time I have seen an animal slaughtered. I think of what a common sight this would have been in ancient Roman times.

Finally the ram is still. The butcher makes a small cut in the skin of one of the ram's upper hind legs and blows into this, inflating the ram like a balloon. This makes it easier for him to skin the ram, which he expertly does in about ten minutes. About halfway through the skinning process Mohammed and his brother help carry the ram to the vestibule of the house. The ram is strung up from a hook on a beam so that all the blood will drain away into a plastic tub underneath. As the elder finishes skinning the ram, Mohammed invites us to stay and eat with his family. 'We make kebabs of the heart and kidneys,' he says. 'And tomorrow we will eat his head with couscous.'

We thank him but say we would now like to continue with the tour of mountain Berbers.

LOST IN MARRAKECH

EXCERPTS FROM THE BLUEBERRY-COLOURED NOTEBOOK:

SUNDAY 1 JANUARY 2006 – *Marrakech!*

7.00pm? – From the airport we get a horribly overpriced taxi to the old town, near the Bab el Rob gate. As soon as we step out of the taxi a boy accosts us and asks us if we need help. Actually, yes, we do. He helps us find our riyadh in the maze of streets. I tip him a couple of English pounds. He seems disappointed. We dump our bags, take minimum money and set out for Djema el Fna. The concierge told us it's a 20min walk. The boy meets us again and gives back the pounds. I say I'll try to change them.

7.45pm – We get a taxi to Djema el Fna. The famous square of Marrakech is crowded with beggars, snake charmers, acrobats, storytellers and street musicians. One man is playing a lyre-like instrument and wearing a live white rooster on his head. He is bouncing gently up and down.

8.00pm – The food stalls create a cloud of smoke over the square, which is lit by bright white lights. We have a bowl of harira (thick soup) at a bench. It has vegetables and noodles. It costs about 50p for two bowls. Then we have a drink of something which we think is mint tea but turns out to be hot ginseng! I see the assistant washing the used glasses in a barrel of water and then wiping them with a grimy tea towel. Yikes!

8.20pm – We walk around and see lots of little hole-in-the-wall cafés. We buy a big bottle of water. We are lost.

9.00pm – We hail a taxi to take us back for an agreed price. When we left our riyadh, I chose a pylon as a landmark. Richard chose a diamond-panelled wooden shutter. I scoffed at his choice but when we drive back down the street I see there is a pylon on every corner, but only one diamond-patterned shutter. The boy who first accosted us helps us find the riyadh. I still have not had a chance to change my pounds. Note to self: get lots of US dollars for tips. The dollar is accepted anywhere, pounds sterling not so much …

· QUESTION ·

WHO IS WARNED IN A DREAM 'DO NOT PASS A BEGGAR BY WITHOUT GIVING' IN THE BEGGAR OF VOLUBILIS?

ANSWER: FLAVIA

DETECTIVE ASSIGNMENT VII:
FINDING YOUR WAY AROUND

What you will need: your brain and a mnemonic technique.

Sometimes you will be staying in a town with narrow, crooked streets and signs in languages you can't read. When Richard and I arrived in Marrakech Old Town at night, I chose a pylon as a landmark and he chose a diamond on a shutter. His choice was better. But three or four landmarks are best. Try to link them if you can. Choose things that don't move and are permanent. So don't choose a car as your landmark or a sleeping cat or even a food-stall. They may all be gone within an hour or two, or less!

Occasionally, if I am exploring a new city without a map, I take photos every so often. I have a digital camera and can retrace my steps by looking at the photos backwards. But it's better to train yourself to be observant and remember landmarks.

Your test: Go away from your hotel or house a short distance. Find some landmarks, especially on corners where you turn. Go back. Now go a little further. Now go back. Go with your parent, guardian or older sibling. Tell them not to help you unless you ask for help. Go as far as you dare. Come back.

You can write the landmarks down if you want in your notebook – or take photos – but try not to look. You are training yourself to remember. Sometimes you can make links, in the same way memory masters make links. For example, in Athens I saw a billboard of a man in a bathrobe. It caught my attention. If that sign was my first landmark and a fountain the next landmark, I could imagine the man in the bathrobe jumping in the fountain with a big splash. And drops from the splashing fountain fall on a fragrant tree with pink blossoms (my next landmark) and some of the blossoms drop off and swirl into a shop with a flickering neon light which sells men's hats, and a hat flies out and lands on the head of a statue, and so forth. Funny or strange images which involve motion are easier to remember than static and boring images.

Be careful! Some things look different on your way back, coming from a different angle or direction. And your story might not work as well on the way back.

If you are in a car, train or bus while you are travelling, you can practise this technique by looking for landmarks and making a story by linking them. Then try to write them down after you've memorised ten or twelve. The more you practise, the better you will get.

TWELVE TASKS TO DO IN MOROCCO (FROM EASY TO CHALLENGING):

1. Learn how to say 'hello', 'please', 'thank you' and 'toilets?' in French.
2. Buy a CD of Moroccan music.
3. Buy and eat a bowl of 'harira' soup in Djema el Fna.
4. Sketch a snake charmer at the Djema el Fna in Marrakech.
5. Visit a souk and buy something an ancient Roman might have used.
6. Watch the butcher slaughter a chicken or sheep.
7. Throw bread to the sacred fish at Chella Castle outside Rabat.
8. Sketch the bronze bust of handsome King Juba II in the Rabat Museum.
9. Smell the tanneries in Fes.
10. See the storks' nests in the ruins of Volubilis, a magnificent Roman city.
11. Visit a Berber Village.
12. Go to a hammam and have a massage.

LIBYA

Libya has only recently begun to welcome tourists and if you visit this country you will almost certainly go with a guided tour group. Richard and I went to research part of *RM XIV*. Our tour group had a British guide, a Libyan guide and a member of the tourist police. (Each tour group needs its own policeman to help pass through the military checkpoints every few miles along the roads.)

Today, Libya's wealth mainly comes from oil. In Roman times, it came from the much-needed wheat that it exported to Rome, along with exotic beasts for the arena. For this reason, most of the important sites in Libya were ports, either Phoenician, Greek or Roman. By Flavia's time they were all under Roman rule.

Libya's ancient ruins are mostly in stunning locations by the sea and are almost all well preserved. But Libya is not as colourful as Morocco or Egypt, and because the Libyan lifestyle is so different from ours, there is not much to do after dark. If you go to Libya, bring a pack of cards, a few board games and some good books to keep you happy in the evenings.

Tripoli is the capital of Libya. Its name comes from

'Tripolitania' which means 'three cities' in Greek: Oea (Tripoli), Sabratha and Leptis Magna. Our tour started in Tripoli with a visit to the National Museum. In addition to dozens of rooms full of ancient sculptures and mosaics, you can see objects like Colonel Gaddafi's turquoise VW beetle and a two-headed calf (stuffed). The birth of a two-headed animal must have been a powerful omen in Roman times.

The impressive Arch of Marcus Aurelius in Tripoli is on a lower level than the streets around. As always, to go back in time, you go down. Our guide took us through the medina and on the way we peeked into some mosques and visited a teahouse built on the site of a small caravanserai.

> The caravanserai was two
> storeys tall and had a blank white wall pierced by
> a single arch. As they came closer Nubia could see
> the plaster was grey rather than white, and
> peeling. Passing through the arched entrance, they
> entered a straw-scattered earthen courtyard
> surrounded by stalls, each one filled with camels,
> donkeys, even horses. On an upper level above
> the stalls were rooms, with a wooden balcony
> running right the way round.
> (RM XIV, p54)

The next day we flew to Benghazi, all the way in the Roman province of Cyrenica, where we met our bus and our bus driver Bahlul, who played the Libyan bagpipes on our last evening.

Using Benghazi as a base, we saw ruins of Greek cities of the Pentapolis (you guessed it: five cities) including Cyrene, a green, well-watered sanctuary to Apollo that reminded us both of Delphi. Then we turned west for the long drive back along the coast to Tripoli, with Leptis Magna as our highlight. It is said to be the best-preserved ancient Roman city in the world, but I found it too big and overwhelming. On our last day we visited Sabratha, and this was my favourite of them all because it reminded me of Ostia. It even has links with Ostia because a corporation of exotic beast importers from Sabratha had an office at the Forum of the Corporations.

Most of the ruins we saw dated from the reigns of emperors who lived in the 2nd and 3rd centuries AD. I have to be careful not to use buildings built after AD 80 in my books. They wouldn't have existed yet! But I had to include the amazing theatre of Sabratha, made of beautiful rose pink sandstone and lots of added marble columns. It is my favourite ruin in Libya.

On our travels through Libya we saw lots of animals: a ram being led to the slaughter, a lost lamb, a mother camel and her baby in the back of a Mazda pick-up, chickens, doves, a tiny dik-dik tottering on delicate hooves.

A glimpse of ancient Roman customs in modern Libya is the way men go out to wait for work every morning. They stand or sit at traffic junctions or round-abouts. In Roman times, labourers would have gone to the town square to wait for work, like the men in the parable Jesus told:

' . . . *About the third hour he went out and saw others*

standing in the market place doing nothing. He told them, 'You also go and work in my vineyard, and I will pay you whatever is right.' Matthew 20: 3-4

Because the country is not quite geared up to us Westerners, the toilets at the historical sites are an adventure. Many of them are ceramic footprints with a hole on the ground in between. You place your feet where indicated and squat down. It's quite a challenge.

> *It tasted like some sort of date paste mixed with olive oil and pepper. That made it a little more palatable. She tentatively tried one of the pink chunks of meat. It was slightly acrid and greasy. She could not identify it.*
> *. . . 'The esteemed elder asks if you enjoy the lizard.' . . . 'Our food. Is great delicacy.'*
> (RM XIV p96)

Food for tourists in Libya is mainly chicken or lamb, plus rice or chips. But it was the best chicken I have ever had. We were also served the popular 'Libyan soup', which has bits of meat and spices and pasta granules. We hoped the meat wasn't camel-meat; we are fans of camels. If you find the food bland, you can spice it up with harissa, a hot chilli paste.

The 'Egyptian bean porridge' served by some hotels for breakfast is delicious, and has probably not changed down the centuries. Date palms drop their golden fruit onto the sidewalks: ripe and sweet and ready to be eaten. But better wash them first!

Back in Tripoli on our last night, Richard and I wandered through the narrow streets of the medina. Here we found coppersmiths and goldsmiths, as well as cheap clothing, shoes, make-up and henna tattoo sheets (you apply them to your hands and feet). I spent about ten pence on a tiny bottle of kohl, the ancient eyeliner used by Cleopatra. Through one doorway I caught a glimpse of a man creating a shower of sparks as he sharpened his knife. Passing another shop I was stopped short by the mixed scent of cinnamon, cloves and dried rose-petals, all in big open bags along with other spices. And in a café men were smoking apple-scented tobacco in their narghiles (water pipes).

As we explored the medina, some people smiled at us, but others regarded us with suspicion. Once or twice on our trip children had thrown rocks at our bus or called out insults. We western Europeans must seem very rich and spoilt to the Libyans. It occurred to me that as a highborn Roman, Flavia would not always have been welcomed. Some provinces deeply resented Roman rule and taxes.

DETECTIVE ASSIGNMENT VIII: PUT YOURSELF IN THEIR PLACE

What you will need: your imagination and an adult nearby.

Go to a place where there are other Libyans, especially women and children. The medina in Tripoli is good for this. Look out for girls or boys your own age. Put yourself in their place. Imagine you are from a big family, with lots of brothers and sisters, aunts and uncles. Imagine you are quite poor and that you have to help around the house before and after school. Imagine your only exposure to Westerners is through bad American television. Imagine that your teachers used to say all Europeans are rich and selfish, and only concerned with material things, like iPods, designer clothing, mobile phones and computer games. Now try to put yourself in the place of those Libyan children, who have none of those things. Try to stand outside yourself and see how you and your family appear to them.

A good traveller (and a good writer!) should be able to put himself or herself in someone else's place. So should good detectives, because they need to understand people's motives.

TWELVE TASKS TO DO IN LIBYA (FROM EASY TO CHALLENGING):

1. Learn how to say 'hello', 'please', 'thank you' and 'toilets?' in Arabic.

2. Eat some dates or a bowl of 'Libyan soup'.

3. Buy something with a camel on it.

4. Listen for the muezzin's call of 'Allah Akbar!' God is great!

5. Find the two-headed sheep at the museum in Tripoli.

6. Take a puff from a narghile (water-pipe), or sit close enough to smell the scent.

7. Imitate Narcissus the pantomime on the stage of Sabratha's reconstructed theatre.

8. Find the Medusas at Leptis Magna (they turn away evil).

9. Use a two-feet-and-a-hole toilet.

10. Copy a Greek or Roman inscription in your notebook.

11. Visit the amazing bread-like oasis city of Ghadames.

12. Make friends with a Libyan and get yourself invited to their home for dinner. (If you achieve this last task, email me and tell me all about it!)

EGYPT

Egypt! Land of pyramids, pharaohs and papyrus. Land of cats, crocodiles, curses and Cleopatra. For my fifteenth book, I wanted Nubia to return to her home country, and I also wanted to show our friends travelling up the Nile. So I booked a Nile cruise for the end of May, the month Flavia et al. will be travelling. Richard and I flew to Luxor, (ancient Thebes), then boarded an ancient paddle steamer – like the one in *Death on the Nile* – to Aswan and back.

Sailing at only three miles per hour, you can really see the life on the banks of the Nile, unchanged over four thousand years. Men in their long, loose tunics and turbans cutting alfalfa for their donkeys, boys casting their nets from little boats, women getting water in pots, people washing clothing and themselves. On the banks you see water buffalo, mules, reed huts and mud villages. Although it is desert beyond, the banks of the Nile are very lush. A Roman traveller would have recognized date palms, acacias, papyrus, mimosa and sycamore, but not the banana plants, sugarcane, pampas grass, or mangos.

We see the big granite sculpture of a falcon and stand under rays of light at the Temple of Horus at Edfu. I make note of mummified crocodiles and a secret passage at Kom Ombo. We see bats flitting in the dusk on the island temple of Philae, where there is a sound and light show. We see the amazing carved reliefs of Pharaohs and animal-headed gods striding across monumental walls of tombs and temples. Traces of paint show they would once have been painted in colours as bright as those in modern comic-books. I love the hiero-glyphs and want to learn to translate them immediately. I can soon identify the signs for Sun of Ra (a duck and a disc) and the signs for 'Land of Sedge and Bee.'

The monuments are awe-inspiring, but what fasci-nates me more are traces of life as it would have been. So instead of going to Abu Simbel, we opt for a bird watching cruise around the islands of Aswan. After all, birds are birds. Our guide Arabi is a native of this town and has taught himself about birds and plants. He points out the hooded crow, swallows, parakeets and 'loving doves'. He shows us how to differentiate the great egret from the cattle egret. We also see a purple heron and lots of moorhens, which I guess are from Africa since 'moor' comes from 'Mauretania'. There are also green bee-eaters and little bittern, but we don't see those this day. Arabi claims the Nile is so clean you can drink from it. He demonstrates! He helps us identify papyrus, date palms, a kind of acacia called the wattle-tree that grows close to the water. My book will be set in May so I make note of everything now in bloom: the mimosa has little pink flowers and the wattle tree has yellow blossom.

At the end of our bird and plant tour, we stop at an island

to visit to a Nubian village. Although it is baking hot outside, inside the Nubian house it is very cool. The plastered walls are covered with colourful and primitive designs. Of course, the Nubians used to be mainly nomadic, but since all their land was flooded by the high dam in 1960, they have been re-located to houses in and around Aswan. Arabi hands a live baby crocodile to Richard, who describes it as feeling bumpy on the back but with an underbelly soft as a kitten's. We are served mint tea and I get a 'Nubian henna' design on my hand. Later I discover this can be dangerous if the henna they use is not of the highest quality. Outside I photograph an old man with his donkey cart, a spice-seller at his stall and a poor Nubian family.

On our next to last day we take a hot air balloon ride over the Valley of the Kings. It is terrifying and beautiful, and as the sun rises, it casts the shadow of our balloon on the barren hills. We land at 8.15am to find the valley already packed with tourists. A Disneyland style-train takes us up to the entrances, but the Valley of the Kings is like a stone quarry, with no shade and the lofty stone walls pound back the heat. It is not even cool inside the tombs, as you might expect. 'This is not crowded at all,' says Ahmed, as we pile back on the air-conditioned coach. 'You should see it in February and March.' We endure one more blistering monument, the tomb of Hatshepsut, then run for the café and a cool drink.

For our last morning, we visit Karnak and Luxor Temple, with a papyrus factory sandwiched in between. I watch the demonstration of how papyrus is cut, pounded and pressed, then a modern 'scribe' writes Flavia, Jonathan, Nubia and Lupus in hieroglyphic letters. This Scribe of Luxor has given me even more ideas for *RM XV*!

TWELVE TASKS TO DO IN EGYPT (FROM EASY TO CHALLENGING):

1. Learn to read the Egyptian Arabic numbers from one to ten.

2. Learn some basic hieroglyphics – 'Son of Ra' is a duck followed by a disc.

3. Try a glass of mint tea – very sweet and very hot.

4. Wear Egyptian clothing for a whole day. If you haggle, you can buy a whole outfit – loose tunic and sandals – for under £10.

5. Go for a felucca trip on the Nile.

6. Try Egyptian porridge for breakfast; it's made of beans.

7. Visit a papyrus factory to see how papyrus is made, watch a 'scribe' write your name in hieroglyphics.

8. Look at the stars at night and see if you can find the constellation Nubia calls 'the big camel'.

9. Hold a live baby crocodile in the Nubian village at Aswan.

10. Ride a camel.

11. Visit the new library at Alexandria.

12. Ride a hot air balloon over the Valley of the Kings.

SAILING UP THE NILE

EXCERPTS FROM THE RASPBERRY-COLOURED NOTEBOOK:

TUESDAY 22 MAY 2007 – *S.S. Karim on the Nile from Luxor to Aswan*
Our handsome young guide Ahmed gives us a briefing in the brass and teak lounge of the ship: Watch out for scams, he tells us. One scam is that a seller will try to give you change in 'Nubian pounds' instead of Egyptian pounds. There is no such thing as a 'Nubian pound'. Don't buy cheap perfume from the market. It is made of food oil and you will end up smelling like an omelette.
Idea: the air was so dry that Flavia couldn't smell anything, just the occasional musky whiff from the tiller man's armpits, or a hint of wet hempen rope.
5.00pm – On the way to Kom Ombu
A small donkey trotting purposefully in a cloud of his own dust, the cloud golden in the late afternoon sunset. His rider's feet almost touch the ground.

WEDNESDAY 23 MAY 2007
10.15am – Very hot out there but cool under the split reed awning of the deck … lush palm groves on the bank, first one side, then the other …
3.00pm – Aswan
A felucca is the timeless boat with a distinctive triangular sail. Like most of the feluccas here at Aswan, the owners were Nubians. The boy at the tiller has lovely features and neat ears, his skin a mid brown

rather than pale like Egyptians or ebony like Ethiopians. At the
end of our trip he picks up a tambourine and sings for us.

THURSDAY 24 MAY 2007 – *Aswan*
We go with Steve and Sue to see the Aswan granite quarry
and the famous unfinished obelisk. Steve is a stonemason from
Dudley and he bounds around the rocks like a kid in a candy
shop. 'Why didn't I bring my rock-chisel?' he moans. Later, back
at Karnak, he buys three little alabaster statues for about £5:
an ibis, a cat and a sphinx. Quite a good deal. But when he
gets on the bus he discovers they are wax! The stonemason
confounded.

SATURDAY 26 MAY 2007 – *Edfu*
7.40am – Two sleepy-eyed donkeys – one grey, one mace –
pull a four-wheeled cart with five boys in it.

SUNDAY 27 MAY 2007 – *Luxor*
8.20am – Valley of the Kings and HOT... in preparing a
mummy the first cut is made in left hand side because jackals
devour their prey from left hand side ... Anubis is the jackal-
headed god of the dead ... If you follow the principles of Mat you
will go to heaven. Body goes to jury ... heart is weighed, it has to
equal the sacred feather ... underground tomb painted with ochre,
lapis lazuli, etc, then coated with beeswax to protect painting ...
Greeks called these tombs 'syringes' or 'pan pipes' ... Decoration on
walls could be considered a guide book ... at each doorway the
demi-god would pose a riddle. The dead person had to answer it
correctly, or it was the permanent end of his life: In fact all life. The
sun would not rise, the Nile would not flood, the moon would not

wax ... If dead Pharaoh came to a locked door and could not answer the gatekeeper's riddle, he could just look to the right. Idea: Flavia or Nubia has a dream that they come to door and are posed a riddle. They try to look right but ...

DETECTIVE ASSIGNMENT IX: SCENTS AND SMELLS

What you will need: your nose.

See how many smells you can list in a day. You can do this anywhere. But it's especially fun in countries like Egypt where there are exotic spices and other interesting smells. Try to describe the scents you have never smelled before. For example, to someone who has never smelled mastic, I describe it as a cross between carrot and cumin.

· QUESTION ·

IN WHICH OF MY BOOKS DOES FLAVIA SMELL SOMEONE'S SCENT IN A ROOM, AND THEN WHEN SHE RUNS TO HIDE, THE PERSON WHO ENTERS SMELLS *HER*?

ANSWER: THE SIRENS OF SURRENTUM, P103

DETECTIVE ASSIGNMENT X: COMING HOME

What you will need: a fresh point of view and your notebook.

An amazing thing about travelling is that when you get home, you see everything with 'new eyes'. When you get back from your trip, pretend you are arriving in your home town for the first time. Try to observe your 'familiar world' with the same focus and concentration you put into making observations on your first day in another country. Take note of the smells, the sounds, the language, the way the people dress and look, the music you hear, the air, the light, the birds, the animals, the cars, the street signs, the whole flavour of the place. Pretend you are from ancient Rome coming to your town. What would it look like to a Roman?

CAROLINE'S POST SCRIPTUM (P.S.)

I hope this guide has made you eager to travel and use your powers of imagination and observation, maybe even to write a story based on your travels. If you make any exciting discoveries, please send me one care of:

Orion Children's Books,
5 Upper St Martin's Lane,
London, WC2H 9EA

or email me at:

flaviagemina@hotmail.com

And don't forget: you can find lots more information on the books and the places they are set at the official Roman Mysteries website:

www.romanmysteries.com

Cura ut valeas! (Take care to keep well!)

Caroline

USEFUL WEBSITES

Official Roman Mysteries website:
http://www.romanmysteries.com

Best Ostia website:
http://www.ostia-antica.org

Official Ostia website:
http://www.itnw.roma.it/ostia/scavi

Visiting Laurentum:
http://www.romanmysteries.com/books/LaurentumVisit1.htm

Wildlife of Laurentum:
http://www.romacivica.net/cyberia/riserva/efusano.htm

Visiting Isola Sacra:
http://www.romanmysterics.com/books/isolasacravisit1.htm

The Golden House:
http://www.romeguide.it/domus_aureaeng/domus_aurea.htm

Villa Limona:
http://www.romanmysteries.com/books/VillaLimona.htm

Pompeii:
http://www.pompeiisites.org/database/pompei/pompei2.nsf
(With links to sites at Stabia and Herculeaneum)

INDEX

As well as the seventeen novels in the Roman Mysteries series, published and forthcoming, there are other books about Flavia and her friends for you to enjoy. Turn over the page to find out more . . .

TRIMALCHIO'S FEAST
AND OTHER MINI-MYSTERIES

Find out what else has been going on between each exciting instalment of the Roman Mysteries series . . .

If you have ever wondered what Flavia and her friends were doing between each of their adventures, then this collection of mini-mysteries, each complete in itself, filled with extra insights and revelations into the characters' lives, will help answer some of your questions. These short stories bring together all the mini-mysteries in the lives of our four detectives during the dangerous, exciting reign of Emperor Titus.

Includes an exclusive interview with Caroline Lawrence on the secrets of writing mystery stories!

How well do *you* know the Roman Mysteries?

As well as being gripping adventures, Caroline Lawrence's bestselling novels are packed with facts about ancient Roman life. Test your knowledge in these books for all Roman Mysteries fans, and anyone fascinated to know what life in first-century Rome was really like.

THE FIRST ROMAN MYSTERIES QUIZ BOOK

This quiz book includes 500 questions on each of the first six mysteries: *The Thieves of Ostia*, *The Secrets of Vesuvius*, *The Pirates of Pompeii*, *The Assassins of Rome*, *The Dolphins of Laurentum* and *The Twelve Tasks of Flavia Gemina*.

Plus . . . quizzes about Roman Food, Music, Writers and Writings, Ships and Seafarers, Clothes and Fashion, and picture puzzles to solve.

THE SECOND ROMAN MYSTERIES QUIZ BOOK

This quiz book includes 500 questions based on the following six titles: *The Enemies of Jupiter*, *The Gladiators from Capua*, *The Colossus of Rhodes*, *The Fugitive from Corinth*, *The Sirens of Surrentum* and *The Charioteer of Delphi*.

Plus . . . quizzes about Roman Entertainment, Rules and Rituals, Architecture, Medicine, Love and Marriage, and picture puzzles to solve.

THE ROMAN MYSTERIES TREASURY

Here is the ultimate treasure trove for devotees of the Roman Mysteries – for fans of Caroline Lawrence's bestselling books, the highly-acclaimed CBBC TV series, or both!

Flavia Gemina has decided to write a book and has enlisted the help of her friends and family. So join Flavia, Jonathan, Lupus, Nubia and other favourite characters on a behind-the-scenes journey into Roman life during the reign of Emperor Titus.

Find out about sport and leisure, food and drink, fashion and beauty, slaves and freeborns, death and burial, architecture and politics. Read about the eruption of Vesuvius and discover quirky facts about Roman emperors. Plus find out how Caroline Lawrence conducts her rigorous research for each book.

With brand-new maps, insightful, lively text by Caroline Lawrence and stunning full-colour photographs from the TV series, this is a book to return to time and again.

THE ROMAN MYSTERIES OMNIBUS

Join Flavia Gemina, a Roman sea captain's daughter, Jonathan, her Jewish neighbour, Nubia, the African slave-girl, and Lupus, the mute beggar boy, on three exciting adventures in ancient Rome.

In *The Thieves of Ostia*, the four friends get on the trail of the killer who is silencing the town's watch-dogs. Not long after solving this mystery, *The Secrets of Vesuvius* finds them relaxing near Pompeii. When Mount Vesuvius erupts, they flee one of the greatest natural disasters of all time. Sheltering in the refugee camps following the eruption, they discover that children are being kidnapped from the camps in *The Pirates of Pompeii*. Determined to find out who is responsible, the friends come face to face with pirates and slave-dealers . . .

THE ROMAN MYSTERIES OMNIBUS II

Ancient Rome, four young detectives in three thrilling mysteries.

The Assassins of Rome: Jonathan has disappeared on a secret quest to Rome. To track him down, his friends must enter Nero's Golden House, and find an assassin.

The Dolphins of Laurentum: A sunken wreck full of treasure seems to be the answer to the four detectives' problems. As they try to recover it, they solve the terrible secret of Lupus's past . . .

The Twelve Tasks of Flavia Gemina: In order to save her father from a terrible fate, Flavia must perform twelve tasks, just like the Greek hero Hercules.